ROCK HAPPY 3

Discordant

Chris Spence

Table of Contents

Prologue

The bullet struck the branch above his head, showering him in splinters. He pressed himself against the tree trunk, waited for one second, two, three, before slipping his gun round the rough bark and squeezing the trigger.

Fzzoom!

His Mark 2 laser-pistol lit up the early morning air. A millisec later, it was joined by a score more as twenty of his elite squad started shooting.

A fusillade of shots rang out as the defenders returned fire. One foe even had an old machine gun, the *rat-tat-tat* of its bullets crashing into trees and foliage. But these ancient weapons were no match for his troops' modern military hardware.

Whump! Whump!

As more blasts lit up the semi-darkness, his platoon's laz-cannon struck, pulverizing part of the wooden stockade where their enemies sought vainly to hide.

"You should have surrendered when you had the chance," he muttered to himself as the first screams rent the air.

Ten minutes later, General Slade Arnold stood inside the stockade staring down at his last surviving adversary. He was young, Arnold noticed, probably still a teenager. Smoke was curling from his patched-up woolen jacket where the laser had struck him, burning a hole through to his skin. His eyes were closed and his arms and legs were splayed out at odd angles. An old shotgun lay just beyond reach.

"Are you sure he's only stunned?" Arnold asked the soldier next to him as he surveyed the motionless figure.

"Yes, General," replied Captain Cornwallis.

"And the others?"

"Dead, General."

"Shame."

"General?"

"It's a shame they didn't surrender. We could have ..." He trailed off. Why was he bothering to explain? What did it matter? He surveyed the devastation; the limp, lifeless bodies scattered around the burning stockade. His eyes alighted on an old sign hanging at an odd angle above the doorway: "McCullough's Militia. Liberty or Death!"

They'd got their wish, he supposed. First liberty, now death. But why was he here, he asked himself for the hundredth time. Why did the President think John Locke was holed up in one of these off-grid communities dotted among the country's forests and wildernesses? No way would the old man seek refuge somewhere like this. Not after what had happened in Hope. He knew it. President Davison must know it. So why had she ordered his troops to search here?

And why had she ordered him to lead the hunt himself? This kind of operation should be assigned to a more junior officer. The President was aware of that. But she had instructed him, General Arnold, to take care of this personally. Had she lost her faith in him? Her trust? Did she want him out of Washington, D.C.? If so, why?

General Arnold's thoughts turned unbidden to that ambitious young upstart, Colonel Tarleton, who had wormed his way onto the White House staff. Had he been causing trouble? Or perhaps Senator Howe was making more mischief? Whatever was going on, he needed to get back to his country's capital soon.

"Your orders, General?" Captain Cornwallis asked, snapping Arnold out of his reverie.

"Search the compound for clues," Arnold replied, sighing inwardly. "Prepare the prisoner for transportation and call in the helicopters. We leave in thirty minutes."

1 | Running

Alex was running. His breath was coming in hard gasps, his mouth pluming white mist into the cold winter air. He passed the finish line and started another lap. Coach Elkins barked out his time as he rushed by. Only three laps to go. His pace was good and he was way ahead of the others, which helped. Now he didn't have to think so much about running and could let his mind turn to more important things.

It had been three days since his memories had returned. Three days since Alex had remembered his first meeting with the MeChip's inventor, Dr. John Locke, and his discovery that the MeChip—the technology he'd always loved—was being used to control people. He could now recall everything about their plan to disable people's MeChips using music, one of its few vulnerabilities; their success in liberating some of Lincoln's townsfolk at the Best Band contest; and their flight to the forest as they were pursued by the henchmen of General Arnold, Locke's nemesis. Alex could recollect the disturbing secrets that had emerged in the forest as the MeChip's insidious hold on their minds and memories began to loosen. Finally, he could recall in detail their success in finding the sanctuary of Hope, the off-grid community that had offered them shelter and supported their plans to defeat the MeChip by broadcasting music to the entire country. America would already be free again if they had not been captured moments before putting their plan into action.

And now Alex was back in Lincoln, back to his old life, as if none of these other things had ever happened. He was living once more with his mom and his father, whom he now knew wasn't his real dad at all. He was even back at his old high school.

As he ran around the track, he wondered yet again how his memories had returned. Had it happened to anyone else? If so, there was no sign of it. Everyone else seemed blissfully unaware of their adventures: his friends Tom and Sol; his neighbor (and at one point, almost his girlfriend) Abby; his parents; his nemesis Iggy; in fact, everyone involved. It was like everything connected with the Best Band contest and their experiences in the forest had never happened.

One of the only differences now was that Alex and his friends had decided to quit playing music and take up track and field. This, he realized, was almost certainly a result of the MeChip's influence. After all, if General Arnold knew that the right sort of music was a threat, making the people who were in on the plot develop a distaste for playing an instrument made perfect sense.

Alex had noticed only a handful of other changes so far. For a start, Sybil, one of Abby's friends, had not come back to school. Oddly, no one else seemed to have noticed or even remembered she existed. Also in this new "normal" Iggy was no longer dating Abby. That was a relief, but was also pretty weird, now Alex thought about it.

So how had he, Alex, regained his memories when no one else had? As he continued to run around the track, he raised a hand to the back of his neck and carefully touched the skin where the MeChip was secured. It was definitely in there, with its rose-tinted visions and insidious lies still busily gnawing away at his consciousness.

When his memory had returned, Alex had wondered if the people controlling the MeChip would realize something was wrong. For the first 24 hours, he'd been terrified the Fixers would break down his door and drag him away for further reprogramming or, worse still, brain surgery. But nothing had happened. This meant, he supposed, that for the time being they didn't know that *he* knew what the MeChip was really doing. As he continued to jog around the track, he could still see the rose-tinted MeChip-version of the world. Nothing had changed, really, except his awareness of what it was doing to his mind.

Alex thought about his first instinct when his memory had returned. For a few minutes, he'd been tempted to rip out the MeChip and run, literally, for the hills. He'd had some wild notion about fleeing to Locke's old cabin in the woods, taking refuge there before figuring out what to do next.

But going off-grid wouldn't work, not if he was to achieve his ultimate goal. Almost as soon as his memories had returned, Alex had known that his only real choice—his single purpose—must be to find John Locke and defeat the MeChip. Nothing had changed. The evil of that technology, and the people wielding it, had not gone away. Someone had to do something about it. And Alex had read in the newspaper that Locke had escaped prison. He was out there somewhere. Alex just needed to find him.

But how could Alex find Locke? That was the hard part. After hours of thinking, he'd developed the outline of a plan. Sure, some of the details were still a bit hazy. But he knew it would need three stages and he was almost ready to start stage one. He just had to—

"Franklin, what the smeck are you doing?!"

Alex looked up, his train of thought broken as his attention snapped back to the present. Coach Elkins was just thirty paces ahead of him, standing by the finish line and gesticulating wildly. Alex realized he'd been so lost in thought his pace had slowed. Before he could react someone flew past him, brushing against his shoulder. Desperately, Alex put on a burst of speed ... too late. Tom's lanky frame flashed over the finish line half a yard ahead of him.

"Yes!" Tom declared, a triumphant grin on his face.

"What the smeck was that, Franklin?" Coach Elkins yelled, looking at an old-fashioned stopwatch hanging from his neck.

"Sorry Coach. I lost concentration," Alex panted.

"You're twelve seconds off your PB for the 3000 meters. You were moving like a tortoise on that last lap. You let Hamilton beat you and he's a 10k specialist. 10k!"

"I know, Coach, I—"

"Not 3k!"

"Yes, Coach, I said I'm—"

"Do it again."

"What?"

"I said do it again. And if you don't shave at least six seconds off that pathetic result, I'll make you run it a third time, and a fourth if I have to."

"But coach, I've got class—"

"I happen to know you have a free period next. So get running."

"Sorry," Tom muttered to Alex under his breath. Unfortunately, Coach Elkins heard him.

"What are you apologizing for, Hamilton? You just beat him, for smeck's sake. You should be happy. Why aren't you happy, Hamilton? And you, Franklin, why aren't you running yet? I'm starting the stopwatch right now!"

As Alex started jogging again he tried to tune out Coach Elkins' yells but they were audible even from across the track as he continued to berate Tom and Alex in equal measure.

2 | Control

"So you're not coming?" Tom asked Alex for the third time. "But we go to the Happy Store after school every Friday. Why not today?"

"I told you. I need to work on something at home."

"You're not mad at me about the race, are you?"

"Definitely not. You deserved to win," Alex said, trying to reassure his friend.

"Don't tell him that," Sol groaned. "His ego's inflated enough already."

"It is not," Tom protested. "But you really should come along, Alex. Sally and Martha might be there and I'm smeckin' sure Martha likes you. Don't you think, Sol?"

"Maybe."

"Sorry, guys, but I really need to get home tonight," Alex replied. "See you Sunday?"

"Sure."

They parted in front of the school, Alex going one way, Sol and Tom the other.

"Do you think Sally likes me?" Alex heard Tom ask Sol from down the street. "I'm thinking of asking her to the Valentine's Day dance ..."

A few millisecs later and Alex was round the corner and out of earshot, keeping up a quick pace as he headed home.

The house was empty, his parents still at work. Taking the steps two at a time, he closed the door to his room and sat on the bed. This was the moment to start on stage one of his plan: gaining control of his MeChip.

He thought back to what John Locke had shown him months before when they were holed up in the old man's safe house. That day, Alex had discovered that a strong mind can block the MeChip's control mechanism and see the world for what it really is, without the rose-tinted view. He remembered how he had fought off the MeChip's influence for several minutes, seeing flowers Locke had put on the table for what they were; decayed and dead, rather than still in bloom. Not only that, but to Locke's surprise Alex had gone a step further, manipulating the MeChip to make the lifeless flowers morph into other objects; first a cactus and then an owl, which had flown around the room. Alex knew he would need to regain that sort of control and go a step further if he could. For his plan to stand any chance of working, he had to be able to control his MeChip and limit its insidious influence.

Casting his eyes around the room for something to practice on, he noticed his open closet. Several shelves of t-shirts, socks, chromo jeans, and other garments were visible. A pair of sneakers and some black pleth boots were poking out under a pile of dirty laundry, while several jackets were suspended above them on hangers. He focused on one of his favorites; a blue retro pleth jacket with white chevrons on the shoulders.

Clearing his mind, he stared at the jacket. Hard.

Nothing happened.

I'm doing this wrong, he thought. How did it work last time? Finally, he remembered.

Once more he stared at the jacket, this time keeping in mind what the MeChip was doing to his vision; the web of deceit it was casting over him.

His vision became fuzzy as the jacket began to shimmer, the image momentarily distorted. For a moment Alex felt faint as the garment flickered in front of him. Then, without warning, it took shape once more and his eyes regained their focus.

And there was the jacket once more. Crystal clear.

But not the same. Sure, it was still his pleth jacket. But it was older. The navy-colored dye had faded into a wan lavender. The glossy material had lost its luster and there was a small hole in one of the elbows. It was as if the item had aged a decade in a few millisecs. Far from being shiny and new, it now looked tatty and timeworn. Even the cool chevrons on the shoulders looked worn and ragged, Alex thought dismally.

Still concentrating, Alex held the image of the shabby garment. As he continued keeping the MeChip's rose-tinted view at bay, he cast his eyes around the room, taking in the threadbare carpet, chipped desk, and squat, damaged chair. He stood up, pulled open the newly-frayed curtains, and looked outside. The lawn was no longer green but brown and yellow, the grass sickly and growing in odd, tufty patches between bare earth. The trees that flanked the street looked leafless and lifeless. A vehicle drove by, no longer an uber-modern hydrocar but now morphed into a rusty old gas-guzzler spewing fumes from its exhaust.

As he observed the scene before him, his neighbor Abby appeared at the end of the street, vaulted over her gate, and strode towards her front door. Without the MeChip's rose-tinted view, her biz-hippie jeans were faded and worn, her pleth jacket and matching banglettes the same. She looked more tired than usual. Even without the MeChip's influence, however, she was still *uber* tidy.

As he stared at her from his window she suddenly looked up. He half-raised a hand in greeting, but if she saw him she didn't show it. She stared back down at the ground, fished in a pocket for her keys, and entered the house.

Why had they barely spoken since the events in the forest? Did she really remember nothing about their time together? Was the MeChip controlling her, making her stay away from him? There was barely any recognition lately when he passed her on the street or in the corridors at school: sometimes just a frown and the barest nod, the kind you'd give to a passing acquaintance; on other occasions, no recognition at all.

The real world began to flicker and his concentration wavered as the MeChip sought to retake control of his senses. He was sweating with the strain of resisting. Finally he gave up, sinking back on the bed and closing his eyes as the MeChip's influence washed over him once more.

When he finally opened his eyes, the room was back to the way it had always been; pristine, modern, comforting. It was more pleasant to believe the MeChip's lies than to see the world how it really was, Alex realized.

Still, he had to persevere. Summoning all his mental energy, he took a deep breath and pushed back once more at the MeChip's control. This time, he broke through almost instantly and maintained it for longer. Encouraged, he began measuring how long he could hold on to reality. By the time his parents arrived home from work a couple of hours later, he had extended his influence to fully fifteen minutes.

"Are you alright, Alex? You're sweating like you've just run a marathon," his mom said, looking at him closely as he entered the kitchen.

"I'm fine," he lied. "Just a bit tired, is all. How was work?"

"Good, actually. I'm quite enjoying teaching history."

"Not missing your old job?"

"Not really. I thought I would when they announced they were ending the school music program. But it was nice of them to offer me a different role and I did major in history as well as music in college, after all. I guess it's all worked out nicely."

Just then the front door opened.

"I'm home," came a voice. Ben Franklin—or the man everyone thought of as Ben Franklin—entered the room, kissed his wife on the cheek and patted Alex on the shoulder.

Alex forced himself not to recoil, not to flinch at contact with this man who now lived in their house. After all, it wasn't his fault Alex's real father had died five years ago and been replaced by whoever this person was. This man—this stranger—genuinely thought he was Alex's dad. He'd been deceived by the MeChip like everyone else. Alex should feel sympathy, not resentment. Still, it was hard staying calm. Sometimes anger would rise up like a volcano set to erupt and Alex would want to scream out the truth, to confront his mom and this outsider, to shake them both until they remembered what had really happened.

But what good would that do? With their MeChips controlling them, they wouldn't believe him. Probably they'd think he'd gone crazy. Besides, the MeChips had audio devices installed. Locke had told him that. It was all very well thinking things, since the MeChip couldn't read your innermost thoughts. But it could hear anything you said out loud. Not only that, but it was constantly monitoring your heart rate, blood pressure, and other vital signs. Anything he said, or any unusual display of stress or anger, might be noticed by the MeChips' controllers or their AI systems. He had to stay calm and not say anything stupid that might give him away to the enemy.

"How was your day?" he asked, turning towards his fake father and forcing a smile.

Within two weeks, Alex had gained almost complete control over his MeChip. He could hold its influence at bay almost indefinitely, although keeping it going for more than an hour gave him a headache. He could also manipulate what the MeChip showed him and morph one object into another. For instance, one evening he made the chair in his room mutate into a facsimile of the dog belonging to Maggie

Corbin, the old woman they'd met in the forest. The more he practiced such transformations, the better he got.

A couple of days later, something unexpected occurred; Alex began to notice when the MeChip fed new thoughts or ideas into his subconscious.

The first time it had happened, he'd woken around 5:30 a.m. to what sounded like a faint whisper:

You hate playing music. You hate playing music. You love running. You love running.

Over and over again, the message continued to flow through his brain before suddenly shutting off at exactly 6:30 a.m. It was annoying, but he managed to tune it out fairly easily.

What happened next morning, however, was not only irritating but left him feeling faintly disgusted.

He was lying in bed half-asleep when the same voice whispered into his subconscious once more:

You need new running shoes. Go to the Happy Store today and buy new running shoes.

Eww, gross, he thought, as the subliminal advertising repeated itself three times. They're trying to sell me stuff in my sleep? Really?

What was worse, he realized as he watched his reflection brushing its teeth in the mirror half an hour later, was he would have to go along with it. After all, he didn't want the MeChips' controllers knowing he could resist their influence.

It doesn't matter, he told himself as he stepped into the shower moments later. What mattered was that he had gained control of his MeChip. He could not only resist its rose-tinted control, but could manipulate what he saw and even knew what messages it was feeding him.

What's more, there had been no consequences whatsoever. No Fixers had shown up to cart him away. Whoever monitored people's

MeChips, whatever algorithms and programs they used, it was obvious they had no idea what he was doing. Now *he* was in the driving seat.

It was time to start stage two of his plan.

3 | My Chip, Your Chip

Alex kept his breathing regular as he started to reach out with his mind. Concentrating on his MeChip's power, he narrowed his eyes, scanning the air in front of him.

"... differs from longitude, which measures any coordinate from east to west rather than north to south. Keep in mind ..."

Tuning out his geography teacher's monologue wasn't difficult. Mr. Marinus was hardly the most inspiring educator. As the lecture continued, Alex focused on the back of the teenager directly in front of him. For his part, Claude Ptolemy sat staring with equal intensity at the teacher, taking in every single word. Everyone knew geography was Claude's favorite subject. Always had been. Even the monotonous Mr. Marinus hadn't managed to overturn the established order of things.

Alex gazed intently at the back of Claude's neck, reaching out with his mind, waiting for something to happen. For several millisecs, nothing did.

Then a light shimmered, blinked out, shimmered, disappeared.

Alex tried again. Straining every nerve, he gazed piercingly at the point where the light had been. It glowed again, a small spot of brightness at the back of Claude's neck, pulsing slightly before settling into a steady aura. As Alex continued to gaze at it, a small symbol appeared in the corner of his retina: *MeChip 2038CO1941A523.*

He continued to stare, channeling the power of his own MeChip onto the square at the back of Claude's neck where these letters and numbers had appeared. They continued to glow gently.

He turned his gaze towards the girl seated next to Claude. After a few more millisecs, her MeChip code appeared in his vision, too. Claude's meanwhile, was still visible to Alex.

Neither of them seemed to have noticed this electronic intrusion. Claude was continuing to gaze in rapt attention at the teacher, while Muriel was doodling on the tabletop with her finger, staring abstractedly out the window.

Wondering how far he could reach, Alex turned his attention to the rest of the class. Slowly, one-by-one, other necks started to light up with tiny symbols.

Warning! School controls in place.

Alex's heart thumped in his chest as the message appeared in his retina, red lights flashing around it. He forced himself to take a deep breath while glancing surreptitiously at Sol and Tom on either side of him. Had they seen the message? Had anyone else? It didn't seem so.

Then the message appeared again:

Warning! School controls in place.

He let his connection with the other MeChips break off as he took another deep, steadying breath. What should he do?

Without warning, a new message appeared:

Administrator rights available. Accept?

What did that mean? Why were the red lights still flashing around the message? Was that bad? That had to be bad, right?

Administrator rights available. Accept? It prompted him again.

What should he do? Would the MeChip controllers or their AI monitoring systems know if he had administrator rights, or was this something he'd accidentally triggered himself that would fly under their radar? Please let it be the latter, he prayed. Please.

Accept? It prompted a third time.

Alex drew a third deep breath, forcing himself to stay calm.

Yes, his mind replied, hoping he'd made the right decision.

The flashing lights vanished. He closed his eyes ... opened them again.

Everything was back to normal. There were no alarm bells ringing, either inside or outside his head. Tentatively, his mind reached out again to the MeChips nearby. They dutifully blinked back on in his retina, again showing him the MeChip serial numbers of half-a-dozen students.

Wondering what else might be possible, Alex turned his attention solely back to Claude.

Can I see anything else in his MeChip?

Almost instantly, a small display appeared in Alex's retina revealing a ticker tape of vital signs: *Heart rate 75, Blood pressure 120/75, Body temperature 97.8.*

A moment later, a new piece of information appeared:

Level B control mechanism functioning.

Interesting. Alex turned his attention to Claude's neighbor. Within minutes, he'd extended his reach to almost everyone in class, accessing their basic data and MeChip details. Everyone had the MeChip's control mechanism set to "level B". Whatever that meant.

Soon there were only two people he hadn't reached: Mr. Marinus and Martha Skelton, who was sitting nearest the door and in the front row. Was that because they were the farthest away, Alex wondered? Did his influence have a range? He thought back to Locke's old remote control device, which had only worked on the Fixers up to about 20 yards. Would this be the same?

Alex concentrated hard. Narrowing his eyes, he focused on the back of Martha's neck, urging his MeChip to reach out to hers.

"Alex," a voice hissed as someone's knee banged against his own under the table. "He's talking to you!"

Alex looked at Tom, who nodded very slightly in the direction of the teacher.

Mr. Marinus was glaring at Alex, hands on hips.

"Mr. Franklin. I do not like having to repeat myself. If you could kindly stop staring at Ms. Skelton and divert at least a fraction of your attention to me, I would welcome an answer to my question."

"Wh ... what?" Alex asked as the auras around his classmates' MeChips blinked off and he found himself facing one very irate teacher.

"I was asking how you would calculate latitude and longitude for our fine city of Lincoln?"

"Um ..." Alex looked away as he tried to scramble for an answer, then caught Martha's eye. She was smiling at him. He looked away from her, too, suddenly embarrassed.

"I'm waiting, Mr. Franklin."

"I'd ... I don't know ... ask my MeChip?" he replied, hopefully.

Several classmates laughed.

"I've already told you to imagine that the wonderful MeChip cannot assist you on this occasion. Nothing, Franklin? Disappointing, but not altogether unexpected. Anyone else?"

Claude's hand shot into the air.

"Yes, Mr. Ptolemy."

"It's simple, Sir," Claude replied, shooting a superior look at Alex, who tried to sink further down in his seat.

"So why *were* you staring at Martha?" Tom asked Alex as they left the classroom and headed to lunch.

"I wasn't. I was just thinking."

"Thinking she's smeckin' tidy. Huh? Huh?" Tom said, grinning and nudging him with his elbow.

"Thinking that you are a grade A dexter, more like," said Sol.

As Sol and Tom continued to bicker good-naturedly, Alex smiled to himself. Stage two of his plan—gaining access to other people's MeChips—had started well. Now to test how far his powers could go.

4 | Flies and Spiders

There's a fly on the back of your neck. There's a fly on the back of your neck.

Alex strained his mind, trying to transmit the message towards Claude, who was once again sitting in front of him. He could feel the energy from his MeChip reaching out towards Claude's. Suddenly he saw it, a thin tendril of light emanating from him and reaching towards Claude's MeChip, which was glowing slightly. His light touched Claude's MeChip aura, groping its way inside.

There's a fly on your neck, there's a fly on your neck ...

Claude didn't move. Math wasn't even his favorite lesson, so it should be easier to influence him than when he was hanging off Mr. Marinus' every word in geography. But so far, nothing. Alex kept trying, straining his mind as his light tried to break into Claude's MeChip.

There's a fly, there's a fly, there's a fly—

Slap!

Claude raised his hand and smacked the back of his neck, then whirled around, narrowing his eyes and scanning the air around him. He didn't even notice Alex staring at him wide-eyed.

The bell rang and his classmates began to rise from their seats, chair legs scraping against the linoleum. Claude took one last look around him, stood up, and walked towards the door.

"For your homework, please complete sections five and six," the teacher said as they started to file out of the room.

But Alex didn't move. He remained seated, breathing heavily but grinning broadly.

"What's up with you?" Sol asked, looking at his friend. "Your face is all red."

"I'm fine," he grinned.

"You sure? You look like you're about to burst a blood vessel."

"I'm fine. Really."

But he was better than fine; he was excited. He had just broken into someone else's MeChip and implanted an idea inside their brain. It had actually worked! He stood up and took another long, calming breath, keen to make sure his vital signs remained regular, already wondering when he could next test out his new powers.

He did not have long to wait. As the three friends turned a corner in one of the school's busy corridors, they ran headlong into Iggy's buddies, Eddy Dent and Eric Block.

"Out of the way, dexters," Eric commanded. "Winners go first around here."

Alex bristled. One of the "fixes" the MeChip had made since their adventures in the forest was implanting new memories about the Best Band contest. In everyone's minds, the end of the contest had been disrupted when a fire broke out started by an arsonist and wanted criminal named John Locke. When the results were finally announced days later, Iggy's band had won again. Alex, Sol, and Tom had finished third behind Harriet's band, Saratoga Redux. While he didn't mind losing out to Harriet, the idea that people thought Iggy had beaten him again really grated.

"If winners go first, you should step aside," Alex said aggressively. "I heard you stank the place out in last Friday's game."

Eric Block grimaced. Everyone knew he'd had played badly last week for Lincoln High's football team. They'd lost 21-17 and by all accounts, the last touchdown had been Eric's fault.

Eric shoved Alex hard in the chest.

"Say that again, dexter," he said slowly. He had an arrogant sneer on his face, as if he knew Alex wouldn't dare repeat what he'd just said.

But Alex didn't feel like backing down. He was done with being humiliated by Iggy and his cronies.

"I said you stank the place out ... loser."

No one spoke. Eric stared at him as if he didn't believe what he'd just heard. Alex was dimly aware of a crowd forming around them.

"That's it, Franklin! Time for a beating," Eric declared, handing his backpack to his friend Eddy and squaring up, boxing-style, to face Alex.

Alex took off his jacket and passed it to Tom, who stared at him open-mouthed.

"Are you sure this is a good idea?" Sol whispered urgently.

"I've got this," Alex replied calmly, smiling. He looked at his adversary. By all accounts, Eric was bigger than him. Much bigger. But Alex didn't care. He didn't need size or strength for what he had in mind. He was ready.

The larger teenager advanced on Alex, drew back his right hand to deliver a punch, then stared at it, eyes wide. Suddenly, he started shaking his fist from side to side wildly.

"Ohmygod! Ohmygod! Ohmygod!"

He was still staring at his hand and shaking it when Alex delivered his first blow to Eric's gut. Winded, the bigger boy bent double, looked at his hand again, shook his head in confusion ... and attacked.

Alex stepped backwards and focused once more on Eric's MeChip. Again, the giant spider Alex had conjured up in Eric's imagination appeared, only this time it was on Eric's shoulder, not his fingers. Eric stopped and began flapping madly at the spider Alex had created; the spider only Eric and Alex could see.

"What's up with Eric?" someone in the crowd asked a neighbor, who shrugged.

While Eric was distracted by the illusory arachnid, Alex landed a second punch to his adversary's stomach, then wound up for a roundhouse to his chin.

His blow snapped Eric's head backwards and he tumbled to the floor where he lay face down, seemingly unconscious.

The crowd fell silent. Alex walked forward and pushed his boot against his rival, rolling him onto his back. Eric lay unmoving, eyes closed.

"Looks like he's out for the count. You should help your friend," Alex said, looking at Eric's buddy, Eddy. "Unless you'd like a beating yourself. Do you want a beating, Eddy?" As Alex spoke, he used his new powers to project a strong emotion into Eddy's MeChip, feeding him a feeling of profound fear.

"N ... no," Eddy replied.

"What's that? I didn't hear you."

"I said no."

"Good. Now, how about some lunch?" Alex said, turning with a grin to Sol and Tom.

5 | Tom's Big Question

"I still can't believe the beatdown you gave him," Tom declared for at least the tenth time as they stretched out after athletics training next morning. "He was well and truly Tysoned."

Alex smiled but didn't reply. He was feeling pretty good about taking down Iggy's friend.

"Where did you learn to fight like that?" Tom continued.

"Just picked it up here and there, you know," Alex replied.

"There was something wrong with him," Sol said seriously, also for about the tenth time. "Eric, I mean. He seemed distracted ... weirded out by something. Didn't you notice?"

"No," Alex lied.

"He was probably just scared of our boy here," Tom said smugly. "Man, our reputations are going to be stellar after this."

"Maybe," Sol said, stroking his chin. "Shouldn't we be heading back? We need to be in class soon." The three of them began walking slowly back to the changing rooms.

"I wonder if this will help my chances with Sally?" Tom said.

"What?" Alex asked distractedly, his mind still on his new-found powers and the incident with Eric.

"Sally. You know. She must have heard about the fight by now. Maybe it'll help me when I ask her to the Valentine's Day dance."

"Why?" Sol asked. "You didn't beat up Eric, did you?"

"No, but Alex is my friend, so—"

"You're hoping to bask in his reflected glory?"

"Not exactly," Tom said defensively.

"I thought you liked Sybil?" Alex said, still distracted by thoughts of what else he might do with his powers.

"Who's Sybil?" asked Tom.

Instantly, Alex realized his mistake. Sybil had not returned to school after the fight in the forest. The others had clearly been programmed to forget about her.

"I meant Sally," Alex said, trying to cover up his error.

"Alright. Then yeah, I do like Sally," Tom said, frowning. Then his face cleared. "She's *uber* tidy. How about you, Alex? Will you ask Martha? She definitely likes you. And your neighbor Abby is her friend. You could ask her to help you out."

"No."

"Interesting," Tom said, grinning. "So a tidy girl likes you but you don't want to ask her out. I have a suspicion our boy Alex here likes someone else. Now who could it be?"

"How about you, Sol? Will you ask anyone to the dance?" Alex asked, changing the subject.

"Nah. I'll be too busy watching Tom make a dexter of himself when Sally rejects him."

"At least I'll try," Tom protested. "I bet you don't even have the guts to ask someone."

"I could ask someone if I wanted," Sol said.

"Prove it."

"Alright, I will."

"Fine. Who will you ask?"

"Now that would be telling, Tommy boy."

"Okay. But seriously ... who?"

"What are you doing up so early?" his mom asked as she entered the kitchen at 6:50 a.m.

"I was going to … um … surprise you by making coffee," Alex lied. In fact, he'd snuck downstairs early to read yesterday's newspaper, as he had for the past week. He was hoping to find out more about Locke's escape, but didn't want his parents knowing he'd developed a sudden interest in the news. If they spoke about it out loud it might alert the MeChip controllers or their AI systems. This morning, he'd heard his mom coming down the stairs and flung the paper back into the recycling just before she entered the room.

So far, though, his early morning research had been a waste of time, he reflected glumly. There had been no mention of the old man or his escape from prison since that first news item weeks earlier. It was as if he'd been forgotten.

"If you're going to make me a coffee, you should probably turn on the machine," his mom suggested, smiling.

"Oh, yeah … right," Alex said, flicking the switch.

"Busy day ahead?"

"The usual," Alex replied. "Training before school. Speaking of which, I should probably go get dressed."

Ninety minutes later, Alex was stretching out again after training. He was standing in his usual spot beside the track, chatting with Sol and Tom.

"Nice running out there, Tom!" shouted Sally, who was sitting on the bleachers a little ways away. Next to her Martha giggled, catching Alex's eye.

"Thanks," Tom called back, turning red. There was an awkward silence. Finally, the girls got up.

"I gotta run or I'll be late for history. Coming?" Martha asked her friend.

"I'll catch you later," Sally replied. "Shoelace," she said, nodding at her feet. Martha hurried off while Sally took her time with the shoelace, looking up in Alex, Tom, and Sol's direction more than once before finally walking slowly away in the same direction Martha had headed.

"What are you doing, you dexter?" Alex whispered, nudging Tom.

"What?"

"You said you were going to ask her to the dance. This is your chance," Alex urged.

"No way. You think?"

"Yes."

"But I'm all sweaty and—"

"She's alone and she wants you to talk to her. I can tell."

"Really?"

"Trust me."

Tom stood up, hesitating. Alex gave him an encouraging shove.

"Hey ... hey, Sally, hold up a millisec!" Tom yelled, chasing after her and closing the gap in just a few of his long strides as Sally turned and waited, smiling.

"Why'd you do that?" Sol asked, looking at Alex. "He'll just get rejected again."

"I don't think so," said Alex, watching Tom's tall, lanky frame as he towered over Sally, who was petite.

They were too far away for Alex to make out what was being said and for a few moments, he wasn't sure his instinct had been right. Tom's face seemed to have turned beetroot red and Sally was frowning. Tom turned away from her for a millisec. He saw Alex and Sol watching them. Alex nodded encouragingly. Tom turned back to Sally and said something as he ran a hand through his straw-colored hair. Finally, she started to smile. Then laugh.

Thirty seconds later and it was all over. Sally was walking once more towards the school while Tom was sauntering back to his friends, a spring in his step and the ghost of a smile playing across the corners of his lips.

"How'd it go?" Alex asked, grinning.

"As expected," Tom said, trying to sound cool.

"She said yes?" Alex prompted.

"Naturally. Would you imagine anything else?" Tom replied, his smile growing.

"No," Alex said.

"Yes," Sol replied at the same time, shaking his head. But even Sol couldn't keep a smile off his face this time, so infectious was Tom's joy at getting a date to the dance.

6 | Revenge

S lap!

For the third time in as many minutes, Claude Ptolemy swiped at his imaginary fly, twisting around in the chair as his eyes darted up and down in vain.

"Mr. Ptolemy, what is the matter with you?" Mr. Marinus asked, eyebrows raised. "You've been like this all week. It isn't like you at all."

"Sir, there's a fly buzzing around here. It keeps landing on me," Claude complained in a plaintive tone.

"Mr. Tubman, do you see anything?" Mr. Marinus asked Sol, who was sitting next to Alex and behind Claude.

"No, sir."

"How about you, Mr. Franklin?"

"No, sir," Alex replied.

"There you are, Mr. Ptolemy. There is no fly. I would therefore appreciate it if you could stop disrupting my lesson."

"But—"

Mr. Marinus cut Claude off with an upheld hand, palm out, as he stared at him threateningly. Claude's eyes dropped and he nodded, cheeks now a fine shade of scarlet.

"Yes, sir," he replied quietly.

It was all Alex could do to keep himself from laughing out loud. It felt so satisfying getting Claude into trouble. Alex was pretty certain Claude had been one of the kids who'd made fun of him after he'd frozen at his first Best Band contest more than a year ago. Besides, Claude was a teacher's pet and a complete dexter. He had it coming to him.

Over the past few days, Alex had made the most of his newfound MeChip powers. He'd made Eddy Dent spill his soda all over his pants in the cafeteria, convinced their math teacher not to give them any homework for the next week, got Claude Ptolemy into hot water with Mr. Marinus three lessons in a row, and made two juniors who'd mocked him in the past trip over their laces and faceplant in the corridors, much to the amusement of passersby. He'd been hoping to bump into Iggy Elgar, but sadly it hadn't happened yet. Meantime, Alex was wondering if his influence over others' MeChips might extend to getting A grades from his teachers. Would that be a step too far? Surely a small trick like that didn't really matter, given that their whole world was based on a lie anyways?

Of course, he knew he should be focused on finding Locke. And yes, he had forgotten to check the newspaper the last couple of days. But until a concrete clue turned up there was a lot of fun he could have with his powers. He needed to practice using his new mind control techniques, anyway. Locke would understand that.

Wouldn't he?

The room was small and dimly lit by a single antique lamp. A man was sitting at an old wooden desk, his lined face lit by the glow of a computer screen. Next to the laptop sat a blue metal box containing what looked like complicated machinery. A single, solitary MeChip sat on a glass shelf on top of the box, under some sort of sophisticated microscope.

As the man continued to pore over numbers on the screen, an old cell phone rang, its tone loud and insistent. Dr. John Locke picked it up, squinted at the number on the display, and answered.

"Yes?"

"Have you finished?" the voice on the other end asked brusquely in such an odd, quavering tone, anyone listening would have concluded either the signal was terrible or the voice was being scrambled to conceal its identity.

"I have the handheld devices working again," Locke replied, looking at three remote control units set aside on a bookshelf. "They're effective up to 20 yards and can be used to disable and influence."

"Good. What about the MeChips?"

"Almost done. They can retain local functionality without being connected to the grid."

"Distance?"

"Ten paces. Maybe fifteen."

"And if they link to the grid?"

"They'd be instantly visible."

"The blocking mechanism?"

"I'll need another two days, maybe three."

"How long will it give us?"

"Twenty minutes, maybe a little more. What about you? How goes it there?"

"Exactly as planned."

"They don't suspect anything?"

"Hard to tell. Hard to know who to trust."

"When can you come out here again?"

"Not sure. How are our targets? Are they ... wait ... I think I heard—"

There was static, then the call suddenly dropped.

Dr. John Locke looked at the phone uncertainly. Had his ally been discovered? Should he try to call back? He couldn't, of course. They'd agreed he would never do that, not under any circumstances. He would just have to wait. Probably it was nothing and they would phone again later. But if his accomplice had been caught, if that person was tortured or chainstitched, if they talked, then that would lead his enemies here. To him.

Locke tried to ignore the little voice in his head telling him to flee the safe house straight away. Running wouldn't do any good anyway. Frowning, he took another look at the numbers on the computer screen and got back to work.

7 | The Dance

"Hey, Tom. See you tonight."

"Can't wait!" Tom called back to Sally across the crowded corridor.

Meanwhile, Martha, who was walking next to Sally, smiled at Alex, who nodded back uncertainly. His eyes darted towards her friend Abby, who was also part of the group of girls, but she didn't look in his direction.

"Can't wait? That sounded a bit needy," Sol said as they made their way down the corridor and headed for their next lesson.

"No, Sol, saying you can't wait for something makes you sound energized and fun," Tom replied, still smiling. "Which I am."

"Whatever you need to believe, Thomas."

"At least I've got a date. I haven't seen you ask anyone to the dance."

"That's right."

"You mean you haven't asked anyone after all? But you said—"

"I mean I have asked someone. You just didn't see me asking them, is all."

"No way! Who'd you ask?"

"Now that'd be telling, Tommy boy."

"Yes, it would be, which is what I want you to do!" Tom insisted, obviously exasperated. "Anyway, I don't believe you."

Sol shrugged, but Alex saw a faint smile play across his friend's lips. In spite of Tom's ongoing entreaties, however, Sol refused to say another word.

"How about you, Alex?" Tom asked, finally giving up. "Are you going to ask Martha? I know she wants you to."

"No," Alex said. "She seems nice and all, but—"

"There's someone else, isn't there? I knew it! Who is she?"

Alex smiled and shook his head, reluctant to talk with them about Abby.

"Fine!" Tom said, clearly frustrated. "You both keep your secrets. But I'll find out in the end."

Alex glanced to right and left as he entered the auditorium. He ran his thumb along the inside of his shirt collar, which was a little tight around his neck. Feeling awkward and oddly vulnerable, he wondered for at least for the tenth time why guys still had to wear tuxedos for these events? He'd feel way more comfortable in his regular pleth jacket and chromo jeans.

The place was already more than half full, the lights dimmed. A DJ was playing some Synthipop number from a few years ago, but only a handful of people were dancing. Alex had heard that Harriet's band, Saratoga Redux, would be playing later in the evening. In Alex's opinion, Harriet was the best bass player in the school, along with Sol, of course. Alex was keen to hear her play again.

He cast around for his friends for a few millisecs before he finally saw Tom and Sally. Like Alex, Tom was in a tux. Sally was wearing a turquoise dress and matching earrings that really suited her. They were standing close together. As Alex approached, Tom said something and Sally laughed, showing her straight white teeth.

With the MeChip's rose-tinted view, they looked like a lovely young couple; nicely groomed, perfectly dressed. Alex knew that if he blocked the MeChip's influence they wouldn't look nearly so good. For a start, their clothes would probably be old and frayed. But Alex didn't want to see that world tonight. In fact, he had let the MeChip's "happier" lens do its thing for the past couple of days. Life was less depressing that way.

"Hey, Alex!" Tom said as his friend approached. "Seen Sol?"

"Not yet."

"Oh, hey Martha, hey Abby," Tom said as Sally's two friends approached. Like Sally, they were both dressed up; Martha was looking very attractive in a scarlet chiffon number that was drawing attention from several boys nearby, while Abby was more understated in a classy black dress. Alex had to admit they both looked great.

"Hi Alex," Martha said.

"Hi Martha, hi Abby," Alex replied, feeling strangely nervous.

Martha smiled back while Abby looked away, a distracted look in her eyes. Alex wondered if she was checking something on her MeChip.

A new song, this one a Rock Shop classic, started as the DJ upped the tempo.

"I love this song! Let's dance," Sally said to Tom, taking his hand and leading him out onto the dance floor, which was starting to fill up.

"Do you want to dance?" Martha asked Alex hopefully.

"I'm more of a singer than a dancer," Alex answered uncomfortably.

"Come on, it'll be fun," she said. Before he could object, she grabbed his hand and began leading him towards Sally and Tom. As they stepped onto the dance floor, Alex saw Abby drift away to the side of the room.

"Sally said Sol's got a date for tonight but Tom doesn't know who. Do you?" Martha asked as they danced. Alex saw that Martha seemed relaxed as she swayed casually to the music, while he felt clunky and ill-at-ease.

"No idea," Alex replied after a moment. "Actually, I'm not sure he really did bring a date. He might just be pranking Tom."

"Why?"

"Tom loves to know all the latest goss. Sol might just be messing with him ..."

The song changed again, this time to an old Retro-Romwave tune. It was a slower number and Martha moved in closer to him, taking one of his hands in hers and putting her other hand on his shoulder. Alex tried hard not to step on her shoes as she guided them deftly but unhurriedly around the dance floor. Nearby, Alex saw Tom lean in to kiss Sally.

"They seem friendly," Martha said, holding Alex's gaze.

"Yeah ... um ... is it hot in here?" Alex asked, running his finger along the inside of his shirt collar again.

"It feels absolutely perfect to me," Martha replied, smiling and tilting her head to one side.

"I'm just gonna get some fresh air," Alex said as the song finally finished.

"Why don't I come with you?" Martha asked.

"No, you stay here. Back soon," Alex said, hastening away before she could reply.

Alex made his way out of the hall and down a short corridor near the right-hand side of the stage. He pushed the exterior door open hastily and took a deep breath of cold air. He definitely needed to clear his head. Walking out the building, he turned a corner ... and bumped into someone hidden in the shadows by the bike sheds.

Correction, make that two "someones." The couple sprang apart guiltily. It was clear they'd been making out. Alex peered into the semi-darkness, straining to see who it was.

"Sol!" he said, surprised.

"Oh ... hey, Alex," his friend replied.

"And ... um ... Harriet! Is that you?"

"I hope so," came her voice. Alex couldn't see her face clearly, but he had a feeling she was both blushing and smiling.

"So ... um ... you guys came to the dance together?" Alex asked awkwardly after a long silence.

"Yeah," they both replied at the same time, turning to look at each other. This time, Alex clearly saw them share a smile.

"I'm just out here ... you know ... getting some air."

"Us too," Harriet said.

There was another long pause.

"We'd better get back inside," Sol said at last.

"Yeah. I can't wait to see Tom's face when he spots us together," Harriet said.

Alex watched, smiling to himself as the two of them walked away, hand-in-hand. Now the initial surprise had passed, he found himself feeling genuinely happy for his friend. Harriet was really nice and her musical skills were off the charts. Of course, Sol had given up music for now. But still, they'd make a great couple. And they'd known each other for quite a while. Alex wondered why he hadn't guessed earlier that Sol would ask Harriet to the dance. It seemed so obvious now.

After waiting a couple of minutes and fixing his collar one more time, Alex retraced his steps. A millisec later and he had opened the door and was back inside. He was walking down the corridor just past the side entrance to the stage when someone stepped towards him from out of the shadows. It was such a surprise his heart skipped a beat.

It skipped again when he saw who it was. Abby was approaching him. She was alone. And this time, she was definitely not ignoring him.

"Hi, Abby. How are you?" he asked, swallowing nervously.

"She's pretty," Abby said, ignoring his question.

"Who? Harriet?" Alex asked, confused.

"What? No. I mean, yes, Harriet's pretty, but I didn't mean her. I mean the girl you were slow-dancing with earlier; my friend Martha."

"Is she?"

"You know she is."

"I guess so. Not my type, though."

"I see," Abby said slowly. "Who is your type, Alex?" She was standing quite close to him now. Alex ran his finger nervously along his collar once more. Why was he feeling so hot again? His mind was whirling and he felt too embarrassed to answer her question. Instead, he stalled for time.

"So ... um ... we haven't spoken in a while. What's new with you?" he asked.

"Not much. I heard you got in a fight with Eric Block."

"Yeah," Alex said, smiling slightly. "I showed him what's what."

"I heard you kicked him when he was on the ground," Abby said, frowning.

"What? No. Well, kinda, I guess. Actually, I pushed him with my boot. But I didn't kick him, exactly," Alex replied, realizing as he said it how bad that sounded.

"And you did that when he was unconscious and vulnerable?"

"Um, yeah, I guess. But it wasn't—"

"And you think that was the right thing to do?"

"He's a bully. Everyone knows that."

She didn't speak; just looked at him with those perfect brown eyes.

"What?!" he asked at last.

"I just didn't figure you'd fight that way. Isn't kicking people when they're down what bullies do?"

"Hey, I—"

"Look who it is. Franklin the failure!"

Alex turned and saw a tall, athletic figure approaching, a superior look on his chiseled features.

It was Iggy Elgar.

8 | Iggy's Ignominy

He stopped just a few feet away from his rival, looking down at him. His girlfriend Charlotte Riedesel was beside him, looking striking in a sunflower-yellow satin dress. But her arms were crossed and she was pouting and looking annoyed.

"Hi, Abby. What are you doing talking to this creep? You could do way better than him," Iggy said with a smile as Charlotte glared at him. But Iggy didn't seem to notice. Behind them, Iggy's friends Eric and Eddy emerged from the shadows, along with a couple of Iggy's other cronies from the football team. Eric swallowed nervously as he caught sight of Alex.

"I've been hoping to run into you, Franklin. Been avoiding me, huh? I heard from my man Eric here that you cheated in a fight. Now it's time for payback." As he spoke, he started taking off his tux jacket. Underneath, Alex could see the taller teenager's muscles flexing through his white shirt.

But Alex wasn't worried. In fact, he felt a calm descend upon him as he called up Iggy's MeChip using his new powers. His enemy's chip flashed into Alex's view, visible only to him.

"Cat got your tongue, huh?" Iggy said, rolling his shoulders as he limbered up, ready to fight. Behind Iggy, more people were arriving on the scene, drawn to the drama as though by some sixth sense. Alex caught sight of Tom and Sally at the back of the crowd, while from the side of the stage Sol and Harriet had appeared.

The crowd waited for Alex to say something but he remained silent, smiling nonchalantly as his powers wormed their way inside his enemy's MeChip. Inside his enemy's brain.

"Alright, let's do this," Iggy said, frowning at his adversary's refusal to respond. He stepped forward, fists raised ... and stopped. An odd look crossed his face. His brows furrowed, his eyes widened, his nose wrinkled and his mouth contorted as if he'd smelled something rotten.

He lifted a hand to his mouth. Without warning he vomited on his pants and patented leather shoes. He tried to turn away but was hit by another wave of nausea. Throw-up splattered all over Charlotte Riedesel's yellow dress.

Eyes bulging, Iggy dropped to his hands and knees, his breath coming in heaving gasps. It seemed for a millisec that he was done. But no; he vomited again, this time over his own hands.

No one spoke for several millisecs. Then a voice cried out:

"Ohmygod, Iggy, what the smeck!" Charlotte shrieked in disgust. She took one look at him, one look at her dress, then raced off in the direction of the girls' bathroom, audibly sobbing as the crowd parted to let her by.

"Charlotte, I'm sorry ... wait up!" Iggy wailed. It took him a moment to stand then he, too, staggered away after his girlfriend.

A millisec later and they were gone, leaving a stunned crowd, a horrible odor, and a sick-stained corridor.

With Iggy gone, most of the crowd turned to look at Alex.

"Hey, nothing to do with me. Unless he was just scared at what I might do to him," Alex said, holding up his hands and trying to look innocent.

"I'm gonna tell Mr. Wells," someone said, rushing off to find the janitor. Slowly the crowd departed, muttering and gossiping.

"That was weird," said Sol as the others drifted away.

"Maybe he can't take his drink?" suggested Alex, shrugging.

"They're serving sodas and juice," Sol said. "I don't think that's what did it."

"Wait 'till people hear about this. What a loser!" Tom declared as he skirted round the mess on the floor, holding his nose.

"It was pretty weird. What do you think, Abby?" Alex said, turning towards her. But Abby had gone.

"Come on, let's get out of here. This place stinks," Sol said.

"And I have to perform," Harriet added.

While Sol and Harriet headed backstage, Alex joined Tom and Sally as they made their way back to the dance hall. Martha was there but Alex avoided her gaze and made his way to the drinks stand. As he looked on, he saw Tom approach Martha and a group of other girls, evidently telling them what had just happened.

As he swigged on an orange juice, Alex felt a rush of fierce joy wash over him. Soon the whole school would hear about Iggy's humiliation. And he, Alex, had secretly been responsible, using his MeChip to control him, to hit him with a wave of nausea so bad he'd actually thrown up.

It was like a superpower, Alex realized, this control he had over people's MeChips. With this newfound ability, it felt like there was almost nothing he couldn't do ... to anyone.

9 | Revenge and Regrets

"What's up, Tom? You look like someone just stole your best running shoes."

Alex sat down next to his friend in their usual spot near the back of the classroom. But Tom didn't seem to have heard him. He was staring out the window, his eyes fixed somewhere in the middle distance.

"Don't mind him," Sol said quietly. "He's just bummed because he and Sally had a fight."

"What about?" Alex asked, surprised. "It looked like things were going stellar at the dance."

"They were. But Sally got mad at him on the bus this morning for not shutting up about Iggy. She said Iggy getting sick isn't funny and she actually feels bad for him."

"Really?"

"Yeah. And to make it worse, Charlotte Riedesel broke up with Iggy."

It turned out Sally wasn't the only one who felt sorry for Iggy. As the day wore on, Alex noticed that while a few people were happy the school jock had made an exhibition of himself, most of the school seemed sympathetic. The general consensus was that he'd gotten food poisoning, which could happen to anyone. If anything, the incident seemed to have made Iggy even more popular than he'd been before.

By the time Alex entered the classroom for his last lesson of the day, he'd decided revenge was not as sweet as he'd imagined.

"Where's Claude?" he asked idly as he joined Sol and Tom. "It's not like him to miss geography."

"No idea," Sol shrugged.

"He was definitely acting weird earlier," gossiped Tom, who was in a much better mood after making up with Sally over lunch. "Weirder than normal, I mean."

"Are you guys coming round to mine?" Sol asked as the bell rang for the end of school.

"I thought you were hanging out with Harriet?" Tom asked.

"I am, but ... you know ... you can come round too if you like. With Sally?"

"She wants to go to the Happy Store," Tom replied. "Maybe tomorrow?"

"Sure. Alex, what are you up to?"

"I think I'll go find my mom. See how her day went," he replied.

The three friends parted at the end of the corridor and Alex headed in the direction of his mom's classroom.

He walked slowly, going against the tide of students rushing towards the exit. Idly, he used his new powers to read other teenagers' MeChips as they passed him, seeing the steady stream of data in the corner of his retina. Finally, he switched it off and allowed his vision to revert to normal. Feeling vaguely dissatisfied, he continued moving against the flow of kids, which eventually slowed to a trickle.

He turned a corner and entered an empty corridor. A door opened and Abby stepped out. She was alone.

"Hi," she said.

"Hi."

There was an awkward silence.

"Umm ... where'd you go the other night?" Alex asked finally. "One moment you were there, the next you were gone."

"At the dance? Well ... the corridor reeked and I needed some air," she replied.

"That was weird, huh? What happened to Iggy."

"Yeah. And Eric."

"What?"

"Iggy and Eric have both been having a bad time of it lately," she said. She was looking at him quizzically, one eyebrow raised.

"I guess," Alex said, finding it hard to think under the penetrating gaze of her chocolate-brown eyes.

"Especially when you're around," she added, tilting her head to one side.

What was she talking about? Did she somehow know about his powers? Alex wasn't sure how to reply. Finally, to his intense relief, her face lit up in a smile.

"I'm just pranking you," she said. "I know what happened to Iggy had nothing to do with you."

"Yeah. Of course. So what did you think of the dance, Iggy's illness aside?" Alex smiled.

"You know, it was pretty good up until that moment," she replied, still making eye contact. Again, Alex wasn't sure how to respond. She was so *uber* tidy it made it hard to think. For a millisec he had a wild urge to use his powers to tap into her MeChip. He might not be able to read her mind, but what if he were to implant a suggestion in there that she liked him. It wouldn't even be a new idea, would it? More like a reminder. And what if her MeChip had been making her avoid him? Perhaps he should even things up a little?

All of these were the thoughts of a millisec. He was still figuring out what he should do or say when someone rushed around the corner, barreling into him and sending him staggering. With a start of surprise, Alex realized it was his classmate, Claude Ptolemy.

"Hey, watch where you're going!" Abby shouted after the boy as he ran past. But the teenager didn't stop. He just carried on running before disappearing around a corner a moment later.

"Speaking of getting a move on, I should dash," Abby said. "Nice to see you, Alex."

She walked off, leaving Alex alone.

That had been weird, Alex decided. First, bumping into Abby like that had been ... what, exactly? And then being almost knocked flat by Claude had been odd, too. It wasn't like Claude to be sprinting down empty corridors. Where had he been going in such a hurry? And why did it look like he'd been crying?

Alex set off again and soon reached his mom's classroom. She was sitting behind her desk silently, although her lips were moving slightly.

"Hi, Mom."

"Oh ... hi," she said, starting. "I didn't see you there. I was just—"

"Using your MeChip?"

"Yes, just marking some papers. How did you guess?"

"Oh, you know ..." Alex smiled. He found it quaint how adults who had lived during the Retro-Before Time didn't seem to be able to instruct their MeChips without talking to them. Even though the MeChip was fully integrated to respond to clear, simple mental instructions, and even though everyone knew this, many older people just couldn't help themselves. Her whispering had been a dead giveaway.

"It's not like you to visit me here. What's up?" she asked, smiling.

"Just thought I'd check in, say hi, you know?" Alex replied. The truth was, he wasn't sure exactly why he'd visited her here. It wasn't like he could tell her anything about his new powers, about his memories, about ... anything. Not without putting them both in danger.

"Alright," she said, looking at him appraisingly. "I was actually going to head home, finish early for once. Do you want a lift? We can walk and talk." Alex nodded as she picked up her bag. Together, they left the classroom and made their way down the corridor.

"So what's going on with you?" she asked.

"Just the usual. You know," he answered, avoiding her gaze.

"I never got to ask you; how was the dance?"

"Pretty good."

"I heard Iggy was ill. Were you there?"

"Yeah. It wasn't pretty."

"Poor guy. And Tom and Sol both have girlfriends now?"

"How do you know all this?" Alex asked, amazed at his mom's ability to keep up with all the school gossip.

"Oh, you know, I have my sources." She tapped the side of her nose and winked.

They trotted down the steps into the parking lot. In front of them was his mom's sleek new hydrocar. For a moment Alex suppressed his MeChip's influence and saw it for what it was; an old gas-guzzling vehicle with peeling paint and more than a few rust spots. Sighing, he let the MeChip impose its rose-tinted view once more. Sometimes it was just too depressing to face the truth.

They got inside and his mom turned the key in the ignition. A moment later and they pulled away. Alex noticed the gentle purr of the electric motor, knowing it was fake. A lie.

"Alex, is everything okay?" his mom asked at last, glancing at him before turning her attention back to the road ahead.

"Yeah. Everything's just fine," he lied, wishing he could tell her the truth.

10 | The Visitor

"**A**ttention students. This is an important announcement. We have just been informed that a very special guest is visiting our school today."

Alex barely registered the voice on the school PA as he sat in his usual spot near the back of class. He'd arrived a few minutes early and had been thinking again about everything that had happened these past few days.

In spite of his new powers, he felt vaguely dissatisfied and just off, somehow. For a start, he kept forgetting to check the daily newspaper for news of John Locke. Then his revenge on Iggy had done the opposite of what he'd intended. And what exactly was going on with Abby? He wished he could read her mind, but of course that was impossible. Several times he'd had these wild daydreams about what might happen if he used his new powers to insert into her brain the idea that she liked him. She'd definitely liked him in the forest ... hadn't she? Would it be so wrong just to remind her of something she'd forgotten; to move things along a little? If only he could talk with someone, share everything that was going on. He felt sure that confiding in his mom or Sol or Tom would help him. But he couldn't do it. He knew that. Discussing any of this would put them at risk. The Fixers might hear their conversation through the MeChip. And that was something he must not let happen under any circumstances. As the classroom started to fill up, he felt oddly alone, as if cut from the rest of the world by an invisible barrier.

"I repeat, we have just been informed that a very important guest is visiting our school this morning," the voice said again. Alex realized it was Principal Ginsburg. Since when did she do announcements on the school's PA?

"All students will proceed to the auditorium at 9:45 sharp. Teachers, please accompany them. And please, please, be on your best behavior."

Was it his imagination, or did Principal Ginsburg's voice sound a little shaky? Alex couldn't recall anything upsetting her equilibrium before. She was normally so calm and composed. Bossy and imperious? Yes. Nervous? Never.

"Did you hear that?" Tom asked as he sat down next to Alex.

"Yeah. Any idea who our mystery guest might be?"

"No," Tom admitted, sounding disappointed he didn't have the latest gossip. "Maybe it's a famous athlete or something?"

The whole class was buzzing by the time their teacher arrived and, as a consequence, she had difficulty keeping them focused. Finally, 9:45 rolled around.

"Miss, it's time for us—"

"I know, I know. Let's—"

"Are you sure you don't know who—"

"I've told you, I have no idea," she replied, sounding irritated. "We'll find out soon enough. Now come along. And please be on your best behavior."

The whole class filed into the corridor, joining the growing crowd as they made their way to the auditorium. Soon their progress slowed to a crawl and it took almost 15 minutes before they finally reached the hall. Alex, Sol, and Tom found spots near the back. As Alex sat down, he noticed Claude was beside him.

"Hey, Claude," Alex said.

Claude nodded back and briefly made eye contact, but didn't speak.

"You know you almost knocked me over in the corridor yesterday after school."

"Did I? I didn't notice," Claude replied, looking away.

"Yeah. And why weren't you in geography yesterday? That's two lessons you've missed now."

"Oh, that. I'm quitting geography, is all. Switching to chemistry. No big deal."

"What? Why?" Alex asked, surprised.

"I don't know. Some weird things have happened in class lately," Claude muttered, his face turning red. "I keep thinking I can feel a ... well, it doesn't matter. And now Mr. Marinus is mad at me."

"That's no reason to quit," Alex persisted.

"It just feels like fate's trying to tell me it's time for a change—"

Alex was about to speak when Principal Ginsburg walked onstage. Instantly the whole school fell silent as she approached the microphone. Even from near the back of the hall, Alex could see she looked paler than usual and appeared nervous. Her eyes kept flicking backstage and her hands were shaking so badly she almost dropped the microphone as she lifted it from its stand.

"Attention students. It gives me great pleasure to welcome a very important person to our school today. A ... um ... very, very important person. We are honored—beyond honored—to have the greatest living American in our midst. Let us all welcome ... President Davison."

A woman walked onstage. She was tall and slender with platinum blonde hair, immaculately dressed in an indigo biz-suit and brown pleth boots. Even from this distance, Alex could see she was beautiful.

She received the microphone from Principal Ginsburg, who took several steps backwards. For the first time, Alex noticed two security guards flanking either side of the podium, impassive in dark biz-suits and sunglasses.

For several seconds there was complete silence. Suddenly, Alex noticed messages feeding subliminally into his brain through his MeChip:

President Davison is a genius. You adore President Davison. You feel so lucky she is in charge.

Now welcome your President. Show her how much you love her!

As one, the entire crowd rose to its feet and broke into rapturous applause. They were screaming and shouting her name, like ecstatic fans at an epic concert or unforgettable football game. Even Alex found himself caught up in the moment. He knew it was the MeChip doing this, knew it was all lies. But it was hard to resist its influence as the crowd became caught up in its adoration of this undeniably brilliant, beautiful leader.

"USA! USA!" the crowd chanted as President Davora Davison looked out magnanimously upon the sea of faces, a smile playing across her lips. Finally, she held up her hands and the crowd fell silent.

"Please be seated," she said into the microphone. Her voice was barely above a whisper but everyone instantly complied, straining to hear her words.

"We love you, Davora!" someone shouted, prompting another round of cheering.

"Thank you. And I love you, too. I love each of you as I love my country. Together, we have made this land strong and proud once more."

More cheers rang out, but not for long. The crowd fell back into silence. They wanted to hear her speak, to eat up every word and every millisec of this experience.

"Some of you may know I am currently on my America Forever Tour, visiting towns and cities across our land to thank you for all you do as we strive to create an ever-more perfect union."

"It's already perfect thanks to you, Davora!" someone shouted.

"Thank you, thank you," she purred, bestowing on the speaker a flash of her captivating smile. "But the pursuit of life, liberty, and happiness can never end. Even if things are good, we can always try to improve them. And we need to protect our way of life against enemies both inside and outside of our beloved country."

The crowd fell silent, waiting for her to explain what she meant.

"But that is a conversation for another time. Today I am here to celebrate each of you and to thank you for making this country what it is today!"

After another round of applause had finally died down, she continued:

"Before I leave Lincoln this afternoon, your excellent Principal has kindly permitted me to spend a little while visiting some of your classrooms and observing you all hard at work. I look forward to speaking with some of you as I tour your wonderful school."

Another burst of cheering erupted as she stepped back and handed the microphone to Principal Ginsburg, who seemed barely able to move in front of this magnetic presence. Alex saw the president lean in and whisper something to her, snapping their head teacher out of her trancelike state.

"Um ... thank you, thank you, thank you so very much, President Davison. And now ... um, yes, of course ... students, you may return to your classes."

Reluctantly and with many backwards glances, people began to file out of the auditorium. As he entered the corridor, Alex spotted a couple of camera crews packing up their gear. But no one else seemed to have noticed. All anyone around him could focus on was whether they'd be lucky enough to have the president visit their class.

11 | The Warning

"I can't believe she didn't visit us," Tom moaned as they filed out of their geography lesson at the end of the morning. "I was so sure she would."

"Me too," Sol said, agreeing with him for once. The three friends made their way in silence to the cafeteria, where they picked out some food and sat down at an empty table near the entrance.

"She's probably gone by now," Tom complained as they started on their lunch. "And I really wanted to speak with her, too. I mean, we're so lucky she's in charge of the country. She's such a genius. Tidy, too!"

"Who's tidy?"

Tom, Sol, and Alex spun around in their chairs and looked up to see who'd spoken. Alex's heart began to pound as he saw President Davora Davison. She was smiling down at them, her perfect teeth showing as she looked from one to the other.

"Um ... no one ... that is—" Tom spluttered, his face bright red.

"No matter. And what are your names?" she asked, her tone bright and friendly.

"Um ... I'm Tom. This is Sol and Alex."

"Tom, Sol, and Alex. It is a pleasure to meet you."

She held out her hand and shook theirs, each in turn. Alex realized the entire cafeteria had fallen silent as everyone stared at this world-famous figure who had just entered the room. He was dimly aware that his MeChip had resumed sending subliminal messages: *President Davison is a genius. You adore President Davison. You feel so lucky she is in charge. You would love to vote for her one day.* It was very distracting, like trying to sit a test with a bee buzzing around your head.

"And what are your interests, boys?"

"We're athletes," Tom said, finally smiling back. "Top athletes," he added, warming to his theme. "Sol's great at 200 meters and discus, Alex here is middle distance, while I'm 10k and above."

"Very good. Being fit and healthy is so important," she nodded approvingly. "Perhaps you will serve in our military one day? We always need athletic young people. What do you think, General Arnold?"

Alex had to stifle a gasp as he saw John Locke's nemesis. As always, Slade Arnold was wearing a dark greatcoat. His brown hair was cut short and flecked with more gray than Alex remembered, as Arnold returned the president's gaze from his hooded blue eyes. Swallowing his panic, Alex fought to appear calm, desperate to show no sign of recognition. Whatever happened, they must not see that he knew this man; must not guess his memories had returned.

"Of course, President," Arnold agreed without appearing to even look at Alex and his two friends.

"Who else is an athlete here?" President Davison asked, raising her voice and turning to face the silent, adoring crowd.

"Iggy Elgar," someone shouted back.

"And is Iggy Elgar here?"

There was a scraping sound as Iggy stood up. Although Alex hadn't noticed him earlier, he'd been sitting just a few tables away.

"And what kind of an athlete are you, Iggy?" the President asked.

"I'm a quarterback," he replied, flashing a winning smile.

"Of course, you are," she said, smiling back and tilting her head slightly to one side. "And a good one, too, if I'm any judge," she added, narrowing her eyes and looking at him appraisingly. Iggy didn't reply; he didn't need to as others instantly spoke for him:

"Best quarterback we've ever had!" declared one student.

"Led us to 10-and-1 this season," explained another as many in the cafeteria nodded their agreement.

"Impressive," said President Davison at last. "Very impressive, all of you." She turned to face Alex and his friends again.

Reluctantly, Alex raised his eyes and returned the President's gaze. She smiled at him for several long seconds, her eyes narrowing slightly, before casting her gaze back to Iggy, who continued to grin in return.

It was obvious to Alex that Iggy's MeChip remained firmly in control, for he showed no sign of recognizing his father, General Arnold. In fact, Iggy didn't even seem to notice the man as he continued to stare admiringly at President Davison instead.

Alex stole a quick look at Slade Arnold. His expression was cold. He was looking at his son, his jaw clenched. A nerve was twitching below one eye.

"So impressive. We will certainly have to keep an eye on these boys," President Davison said at last, looking at Alex again. "Won't we, General Arnold?"

12 | Making Amends

Alex sat on his bed and took a deep breath. President Davison had just been here, right here in Lincoln. Just what the smeck was that all about? Had it just been a coincidence, a part of her America Forever tour, like she'd said? But what were the chances that of all the thousands-upon-thousands of towns and cities in the country, she'd just happen to roll up here? And what about General Arnold? Why was he with her? Did he always travel with her, or did he come on this particular visit for a reason? Had he seen the recognition in Alex's eyes? Did he suspect anything? It didn't seem like it, since Arnold had been staring at Iggy most of the time. But what if Arnold or the President had figured Alex out, somehow? What if they knew about Alex's powers?

Speaking of his powers, Alex thought back on what he'd done with them so far and grimaced: playing tricks on people, getting off homework, beating up Eric Block, and making Iggy vomit. What had he been thinking doing stuff like that? Was this what he should be doing when the country's fate rested in his hands? If the President's visit had shown him one thing, it was that he needed to get a grip on himself.

He realized Abby had been right when she had said he'd acted like a bully. Power was making him mean. A sense of shame washed over him as he continued to sit on his bed staring into space.

Not for the first time lately, he wished he could play music again. Now his MeChip's control was broken, his fingers were itching to get hold of a guitar. Playing always helped him relax, helped him think. But he wouldn't dare try to get his instrument back. Not now.

He stood up and began pacing the room, thinking hard. He needed to sort himself out, get his plan back on track. He suddenly realized he hadn't snuck down and read the newspaper in days. He should start back up straight away.

But he needed to do more than that. Since he'd already gained control of his MeChip and learned how to access other people's chips—which had been the first two stages of his plan—it was time now to begin stage three in earnest. The President's visit had been a wake-up call. It had shown him how close his enemies were. There was no time to waste.

The trouble was, he wasn't sure how exactly to go about it. Sure, he knew what he had to do: find John Locke. But how to do this had always been the weak part of the plan. Reading the paper for news about his mentor might help, but it hardly constituted an actual blueprint for discovering him.

What he needed was access to more information; a way to find out everything he possibly could about where Locke might be now. How could he know where Locke had been spotted if it wasn't in the newspaper? He obviously couldn't start searching on his MeChip for information about Locke, since that would definitely make the Fixers suspicious.

What else could he do? Was it possible the authorities had clues they hadn't shared with the public? If so, was there any way he could access them?

Slowly, the beginnings of an idea began to form. It would be dangerous, for sure. But desperate times called for desperate measures. And what choice did he have? He had to do something.

First, though, he needed to make amends at school.

"Claude. Hey, wait up!"

Claude Ptolemy turned and stopped as Alex jogged up the corridor towards him.

"Oh, it's you. What do you want?"

"I want to talk to you about geography."

"I quit."

"I know. That's what I want to talk with you about."

"I need to get to chemistry," Claude replied, starting down the corridor again.

"The thing is, I think you should come back to geography. You were so good at it," Alex said, trotting to keep up with Claude's fast pace.

"I'm doing chemistry now. And I should get to my lesson," he persisted, walking even more quickly.

"But the geography class needs you. Mr. Marinus wants you back in class."

"Did he say that?" Claude asked, stopping suddenly and looking at Alex.

"Not exactly. But you were his best student and now you're gone he seems in a worse mood than ever."

Claude looked at him for several millisecs, frowning.

"Come on. Please. No one else can answer the teacher's questions," Alex begged.

"Yeah, but something felt ... I don't know ... wrong, somehow," Claude said, avoiding Alex's gaze. "I just had a sense I needed a change."

"Look, just give it another try, okay? It'll be great again, I promise. Come on, Claude ... we need you." Alex smiled encouragingly.

Finally, Claude nodded: "Alright. I'll come back."

"Great! You won't regret it."

"And ... um ... thanks, Alex."

"No need to thank me, Claude. No need at all," Alex replied as he walked back down the corridor, smiling to himself.

13 | Stage Three

Alex took a deep breath, pushed open the heavy metal door, and peered inside. Two Regs were standing behind the front desk, chatting quietly. Behind them, on the wall, was a "Wanted" poster with a large mugshot of John Locke. Under the picture, in large, black letters, were the words: "Reward—One Million Dollars."

"Can I help you, young man?" asked one of the Regs, looking at Alex as he stood indecisively at the entrance. She was around Alex's mom's age, with dark hair and a friendly smile. She looked nice, Alex thought, although her colleague, a young male officer with a thick mustache, was scowling.

"It's alright, we're here to help. What's up?" she said encouragingly.

Alex swallowed nervously. What had he been thinking, coming here? This idea was stupid. Stupid and dangerous. But he couldn't back out now. He was here. Committed. With a sense of urgency, he pulled up their MeChips on his retina, accessing them both almost instantly.

You left something in your car. You left something in your car.

For an instant, the female Reg didn't respond to his subliminal message. She blinked rapidly, shook her head, then turned to her colleague.

"I just have to head out to the car. Can you help this young man while I'm gone?"

"Sure," he nodded, sounding uninterested as she opened a door behind them and disappeared from view.

"What's going on?" he asked. Unlike the other Reg, this one wasn't smiling.

Forget all about me. I'm nothing. You need to use the restroom. You need the restroom now!

An odd look passed across the Reg's face. He grimaced, rubbed a hand across his chin, then hastened through the same door as his companion without another word.

Alex was alone now. Time to put his plan into operation. Nervously, he approached the counter. He looked over the ledge ... and swore under his breath. It wasn't there! He'd expected to see an old-fashioned computer with a large monitor on the other side. It had been in some of the crime shows he'd watched—a computer the Regs could work off together when there was too much data to show on their retina using their MeChips.

But it wasn't there. It must be in their offices behind that door, Alex decided. But how many Regs were back there? Could he really get them all to leave?

Feeling he had no choice, he walked reluctantly around the side of the counter and cautiously approached the door the two Regs had used. His hand was shaking as he reached out for the handle.

Abort! Abort! Abort! Abort!

Alex almost yelled out loud in shock as the urgent message slammed into his brain. But his MeChip wasn't done:

Leave the station now. Abort! Abort! Abort!

He stood as if frozen, his hand still halfway towards the door as the messages continued to assail him.

What the smeck was happening? Who was doing this? They'd just about given him a heart attack, whoever it was. Could he trust them? Or was this something the MeChip generated automatically; an AI-driven response to certain situations? As if reading his mind, the messages continued:

Abort now. Trust us. Please! Abort before it's too late.

What should he do? He was still standing there, panicked and afraid, when he heard a voice on the other side of the door.

"I told you, I left something in the car. No big deal. I'm returning to reception, okay?"

That was enough for Alex. As the sound of footsteps grew louder, he stumbled back around the counter, pulled open the heavy front door, and raced from the Reg station without a backward glance.

He didn't stop running until he got home.

14 | The Mysterious Message

Alex woke up and rubbed his eyes. He'd slept badly, unnerved by what had happened at the Reg station. As he lay in bed staring at the ceiling and wondering for the hundredth time who could have sent him the message, he had to admit it: his plan had been a total disaster. Did he really imagine he could just breeze into a law enforcement office and access top-secret information about a wanted criminal? What if those old computers were just something they had on TV shows? And even if they weren't, what if the computer had needed a password? The whole idea had been plain dumb.

Whether it was a friend or an enemy who'd sent those messages to his MeChip, they'd done him a favor by getting him out of there when they had. If he'd stayed, he'd almost certainly have been caught. But how else could he find John Locke? Where else could he get information on his mentor if not from the Regs?

He was still lying there, his mind straining fruitlessly for an answer, when another MeChip message appeared:

Fifth and Broadway. Southeast corner. 4 p.m.

Alex sat up. What the smeck was going on?

Who is this? his mind replied.

There was no answer, just silence for several millisecs. Then the same message repeated itself:

Fifth and Broadway. Southeast corner. 4 p.m.

The words lingered for a moment, then blinked out of existence again. Alex tried to summon them back, but they were gone. He checked his deleted messages. Nothing there, either. Erased completely.

Had he imagined it? Should he ignore it? Was it a friend? Or could this be some sort of test—some trick invented by the Fixers? He only had until 4 p.m. to decide.

"I still can't believe you and Harriet are an item," Tom said, slapping Sol on the back as he sat next to Alex and Sol in the cafeteria that lunchtime. "You're a sly one," he added, grinning.

"And I still can't believe Sally is dating you ... or that anyone is, actually," Sol said in his usual monotone.

"Hey, nothing you say can put me in a bad mood, old friend. Just look at what's happened this past couple of weeks. Not only did we meet our country's president, but I'm dating the tidiest girl in school. How could life get any better?"

"No, but I seriously like this girl," Tom continued as Sol rolled his eyes. "And she likes ... oh, was that her down the corridor? Back in a millisec ..."

"Oh, smeck," Sol groaned, rubbing a hand across his face as Tom hurried away.

"What's the problem?" Alex asked. "He's happy, isn't he?"

"That's the problem, Alex. He was annoying enough when he was getting his heart broken time after time. Now he's actually met someone, he's so upbeat it's excruciating. And it'll all end in tears."

"Only yours, Sol, if you don't change your attitude. Seriously, you should stop being so cynical. Hasn't having a girlfriend cheered you up any?"

"Actually, Alex—" he began, but stopped as Tom rejoined them.

"Wasn't her. But we've already arranged to go out tonight. Double date?" he asked Sol chirpily.

"Fine," Sol replied after a slight pause.

"Excellent! How about you, Alex? Triple date, maybe? I'll bet Sally would ask Martha for you."

"No, I'm okay. I can't tonight, anyway."

"Why not?"

"Washing my hair."

"Alright," Tom replied, raising an eyebrow. "But I still don't get why you don't want to date Martha. She's tidy. What's going on, Alex?"

"Nothing," Alex replied innocently. "Just dirty hair, is all."

"Fine, don't tell me then. But there's definitely something odd going on with you these days."

Alex walked up Fifth Street cautiously, his eyes alert to anything suspicious.

Nothing.

The occasional car passed by, but none of them slowed down or pulled over. The intersection was empty as he stopped under the Broadway sign on the southeast corner. He looked around him.

Still nothing.

Was this the right place? The message had definitely said southeast corner ... right? He checked his MeClock: 4:00 p.m. precisely. So, he was definitely on time. Unsure what to do, he crossed the street to the southwest corner, just to be certain he hadn't made an error.

There was nothing there, either. Still uncertain, he crossed to the northwest corner, then to the northeast. Still nothing, unless you counted a used soda can on the ground.

Which he didn't.

Finally, Alex returned to where he'd started: the southeast corner of Fifth and Broadway. He looked up at the street sign again. And paused. Taped to the underside of the sign and flapping in the breeze was a piece of paper. Had it been there when he'd looked at it earlier? Cautiously, he reached up, pulled it down, and looked at it.

Seventeenth and Columbus.

Just those three words. He turned it over, but the other side of the paper was empty.

Seventeenth and Columbus. What did it mean? He looked around, but there were still no other pedestrians nearby. Pocketing the scrap of paper, he began to walk home.

Tom was right, Alex thought as he neared his house. There was something mysterious happening. But Alex couldn't have told Tom what it was, because he had to admit: he didn't have a clue what was going on.

15 | My Favorite Song

When Alex woke up the next morning, his thoughts instantly returned to the question he'd fallen asleep to: should he go check out Seventeenth and Columbus? If so, when? Unlike the previous message sending him to Fifth and Broadway, this one didn't have a time attached.

Would whoever was contacting him send him another MeChip message? As the day wore on it looked like they wouldn't. There were no messages at all. There'd been nothing the previous night or that morning, either.

As he sat in the cafeteria having lunch with Sol and Tom, he finally made up his mind; he'd go there straight after school. Making his excuses for not hanging out with his friends for a second straight day, he set off in the direction of Seventeenth and Columbus the instant school let out.

He knew those streets intersected just a few blocks away from Bright Green Mining Company's headquarters. Although Alex hadn't spent much time in that neighborhood when he was younger, it had played a big part in his life lately. Alex thought back to his first encounter with John Locke at his indie tech shop, which had been situated in the shadows of Bright Green Mining's giant smokestacks. He recalled, too, his time with Iggy when they were being chased by the Regs after running into General Arnold and his Fixers while getting rid of some laz-pistols. Neither were experiences he'd care to relive.

The intersection was a good forty minutes from school, so Alex kept up a quick pace as he walked. At first he kept the MeChip's rose-tinted control mechanism at bay, frowning at the old cars, cracked

65

sidewalks, and lifeless trees. As Bright Green Mining's towers got closer, however, he allowed the MeChip's control to assert itself, unwilling to see the worsening squalor or thickening smog as he made his way into this poorer, more industrial part of town. It was too depressing to see the truth.

He eventually arrived at the intersection of Seventeenth and Columbus. There were no clues on the first corner, so he crossed the street. He looked up at the sign once more. Nothing. But when he looked down he saw something. Scrawled in white chalk on the sidewalk was the following message:

Store, 171 @ 5

What did it mean? The last part might be a reference to the time; maybe he had to be somewhere at 5 p.m. But what did *Store, 171* mean? Should he go to a store named 171, perhaps? He tried searching on his MeMap, but there was no shop of that name anywhere.

Could it mean something was stored at a house that had the number 171? Or that *he* had to store 171 *somethings* somewhere? That didn't make sense at all, he decided with a frown.

Just what did number 171 signify? Alex looked all around for another clue, but there was nothing. He crossed the street and checked another corner, then the last one.

If there was another message for him, he couldn't see it.

There was a shop right next to him by the intersection, though. Did the reference in the message to *Store* actually mean a shop? If so, could this be the store referred to in the message? Eagerly he looked at the door, hoping it would have the number 171 on it. But it was number 22. No help there, then.

Perhaps he should go inside? He advanced towards the shop, but it looked closed. He tried the handle, but it was locked. Next, he tried peering through the windows, but the blinds were down. A thick layer of dust had accumulated on the inside of the window sill, which also had several dead flies, lying on their backs with their tiny legs in the air. Alex guessed the place had gone out of business a while ago.

He stepped back and looked at the exterior of the shop again. A large sign bearing the words 'My Favorite Song' was etched in faded, loopy letters above the door. Below, in a smaller font, was written 'Musical Memorabilia and Collectables'.

He stared at these words for a long time, willing them to help him. He had a strange feeling the answer was right in front of him.

Whatever it was continued to elude him. Finally, with a sigh, he turned and walked back to the intersection, still with that maddening feeling he was missing something obvious.

Surely whoever was sending him these clues could do a better job than this, he decided angrily. If they couldn't make it possible to figure them out, then to smeck with them! Did *Store, 171 @ 5* mean anything at all? Was it even meant for him?

He turned back one more time to look at the shop. It was a shame 'My Favorite Song' had closed down, he concluded. It sounded like it might have sold some pretty cool stuff. Unbidden, Alex thought of his own favorite song ... and stopped in his tracks. His favorite song—as anyone close to him knew full well—was a stellar Rock Shop number. And the name of the song was Larchmont Street.

The song was about some place in San Francisco. But there was also a Larchmont Street right here in Lincoln, about a 20-minute walk away. And he'd be willing to bet anything that the Larchmont Street here in Lincoln had a building numbered 171. Checking his MeClock, he saw it was 4:23 p.m. That meant he had plenty of time for him to make it there by 5. Smiling at last, Alex set off once more.

16 | Crossing the Line

Alex was still smiling as he approached the neighborhood where Larchmont Street was situated. With the MeChip's rose-tinted view still switched on, the area looked nice: modern-looking, ranch-style homes sitting behind perfect picket fences and manicured lawns, with tall larch trees flanking every street.

But Alex's smile faded as he turned a corner. Several Regs were standing in front of a wooden blue barrier, the words 'Regulator Line: Do Not Cross', etched on it in white. Alex stopped about fifty yards away. What should he do? He had to continue. He was determined to get to 171 Larchmont Street now, to find out who this mysterious messenger was. Besides, the fact the Regs were here might just be a coincidence. Alex barely knew this area. Perhaps the street being blocked by the Regs wasn't even the one he was looking for?

It was. As Alex got nearer, he saw a street sign bearing the words Larchmont Street and, under this, the number 100. That meant any buildings numbered 100-199 would be on the block the Regs had cordoned off.

Cautiously, he approached the barrier.

"No entry, kid," said a stern-faced Reg, stepping in front of him.

"But I need to go down there," Alex said.

"You live here?"

"No, but my friend does."

"What number?"

"140," Alex replied, not sure why he'd decided to lie.

"Tell your friend you'll see them another time. No entry."

Alex slunk off, continuing down the street running at right angles to Larchmont. He turned back once but the Reg was still watching him, his arms crossed. Alex stepped up his pace as he walked away.

Was there another way onto the street? Alex kept walking, almost bumping into another Reg. She was standing in the shadow of a tree. Behind her, Alex saw a narrow alleyway that appeared to run along the back of Larchmont Street's rear gardens.

"Can I help you?" she asked, her tone much more friendly than Reg from down the street.

"Can I go down this path?" Alex replied.

"I'm sorry, no. That block is sealed off right now. Reg business."

"I just want to visit a friend."

"I'm sorry, but ... hey, don't I know you?" the Reg asked, looking at Alex more closely. With a start, Alex realized it was one of the Regs he'd spoken to at the station; the older one with the kind smile.

"I ... don't think so," Alex lied.

"I'm sure I know you. Where have I seen you before?"

Starting to panic now, Alex suddenly had an idea; pulling up her MeChip on his retina, he began implanting a message in her mind:

There is nothing to worry about. You will let me pass and forget all about me. You will let me pass and forget all about me ...

The Reg frowned at Alex, then looked away. Finally, her features relaxed and she smiled at him.

"Alright, you can pass," she said, still grinning amiably.

"Thanks," Alex muttered.

"Forget all about it," she said in a dreamy voice as she moved aside to let him through.

Alex made his way quickly up the alleyway, glancing back just once to look at the Reg. She seemed to have erased him from her thoughts already as she faced the other way, looking out onto the street.

The walkway seemed like it wasn't used very much. It was overgrown, with weeds and grass covering much of the path and bushes intruding over garden fences. As a result, Alex couldn't see more than a few yards ahead of him. As he advanced cautiously, a question occurred to him; how would he know which house was number 171? Should he pull up a visual on his MeMap? If he did, might the Fixers or their AI monitoring systems see what he was doing and start to suspect something?

He was still wondering what to do when he came to a particularly overgrown part of the alleyway. A large hydrangea bush had taken over the entire path and he had to push through the foliage to get through. Finally, he got to the other side and emerged into a clear stretch again.

But this time, he wasn't alone: right in front of him, their laz-pistols at the ready, were three Regs. And they were looking right at him.

17 | The Fight

"Who the smeck are you?" The biggest Reg stepped towards him aggressively. He was young, with a thick mustache. Alex's heart lurched as he recognized the other Reg from the station. Would he remember Alex, too?

"I said, who the smeck are you? No one should be down here. Not now," the Reg said, looking up and down the lane as if expecting to see others, his eyes narrowed.

Instantly, almost without thinking, Alex used his MeChip to reach out to theirs, saw their vital signs blinking into life on his retina.

I'm a friend. I'm a friend. Don't worry about me, I'm just a friend.

For a millisec, all three looked confused. Then they visibly relaxed. The other two actually smiled and even the serious one with the moustache stopped scowling.

"Okay, friend—" began one, but the serious one held up his hand for silence.

"Did you get the signal too?" he asked. The others nodded and it was clear to Alex they'd all received a message on their MeChips. "Come on," said the serious one. "And remember, approach with caution."

Ignoring Alex, the three turned towards the nearest fence. It was old, wooden, and tall—taller than the biggest Reg—and had a gate in it. The closest Reg leaned forward and pulled up the latch.

"Unlocked," she said.

"Alright, let's go."

The first Reg opened the gate and the three of them crept cautiously into a long, narrow back garden, their weapons held ready. The place was overgrown, with weeds and thick bushes everywhere.

Seemingly forgotten, Alex watched them. Then, on a sudden impulse, he used his MeChip to speak with the serious one who was at the rear of the group.

Tell them to go ahead. Say you'll catch up soon.

The man stopped for a second, then whispered something to the others. The woman frowned, but nodded. A moment later and the other two were lost from view.

What number house is this? Alex asked the Reg through his MeChip.

"171," the man replied out loud.

Alex's mind was working overtime. Whoever was inside probably had no idea the Regs were there. And if the Regs were about to attack, that meant whoever was in the house was probably on Alex's side.

Didn't it?

Give me your laz-pistol. It's perfectly safe. Just give it to me, Alex instructed.

"I ... I ... okay," the Reg said at last, handing the weapon to Alex, who immediately checked the setting, making sure it was set to stun rather than kill.

"What are you going to—" the Reg began.

Fzzoom!

The man's eyes widened as the laser beam struck him in the chest. The blast forced him backwards, although somehow he kept his footing. He looked down at his burned leather jacket, up at Alex ... and slowly crumpled to the ground.

"Sorry," Alex said, feeling oddly guilty as he stepped over his fallen foe and advanced cautiously up the garden path, hoping the other Regs hadn't heard the noise.

They had.

As he emerged from behind a small tree, the two Regs were standing in front of the back door to a house. But they were facing towards him, their guns pointing at his chest.

"Place your weapon on the ground. Now!" instructed the female Reg, her laz-pistol raised.

"Okay, okay ..." Alex complied, beginning to lower his gun while at the same time reaching out to their MeChips with his mind:

Enemy behind you! There's an enemy behind you!

The two Regs spun around and Alex lifted his weapon and blasted one of them in the back. That Reg fell against the side of the house and slid to the ground.

But the other Reg was quicker. Seeing no enemy, she whirled around and faced Alex. Both fired at the same time: Alex's shot struck her stomach while hers caught him on his wrist, smashing the weapon from his grasp and sending it tumbling into the tall grass. His adversary gasped and dropped to the ground, her eyes closing as she fell, while Alex, still conscious, winced in pain. He looked at the patch of angry-looking red skin blistering on his hand and arm, gingerly touching the spot where the laser had caught him a glancing blow. He gasped at the touch.

But there was no time to worry about that now. Trying to ignore the pain and hoping his wrist wasn't broken, he advanced towards the house.

Just as he reached for the handle, however, the door burst open, smashing into him and sending him tumbling backwards. The back of his head smacked against the concrete path and for a few millisecs he saw only swirling lights, yellow and white.

Finally, his vision cleared. Standing above him was an elderly man. He was short, slim, and slightly stooped, wearing a collared white shirt, a purple tie, and khaki pants. He was holding a small backpack; the type hikers use for daytrips. His thinning hair was completely gray and he sported a trim white beard. The rest of his face was heavily lined, as if the worries of the world were upon him. But his piercing green eyes glinted and a slight smile played across his lips.

"Ah, the cavalry has arrived. And just in the nick of time," he said in a deep, gravelly voice as he stared down at Alex.

18 | Reunion

"**J**ohn! Is it really you?" Alex said with a grin.

"Who else?" replied Dr. John Locke as he helped Alex to his feet.

"Were you the one sending me the messages?"

"Actually, no, but—"

Smash!

"That must be the front door. Really, they could have tried knocking," Dr. Locke said as he glanced over his shoulder. "But that is certainly our cue to leave."

The two hastened down the garden path and emerged in the back alleyway.

"Stop!"

The female Reg—the kind one Alex had met earlier at the entrance to the alleyway—was approaching, gun pointed towards them.

"Move and I shoot."

Once again, Alex reached out with his mind, sending a message directly through her MeChip:

We're friends ... just friends. Let us pass and forget all about us.

The Reg frowned and let her gun slowly fall to her side. She ran a hand across her forehead, staring at them.

"You can go ... no ... that's not right—"

We're friends ... just friends. Let us pass, Alex insisted.

"Yes ... no ... no, that's not right. You're lawbreakers," she declared. Slowly, as if lifting a very heavy object, she started to raise her weapon once more.

Then stopped. Her eyes became unfocused and her arms fell by her side for a second time.

For an instant, Alex thought his mind control had finally done the trick. Then he saw Locke was holding something in his hand. It was an old remote control like the one he'd had months before when they'd first met.

"Come on." Locke led them about 30 paces down the alleyway, out of sight of the Reg. He stopped at a gate on the opposite fence.

"What are you doing?" Alex asked in surprise as Locke pointed his remote control at Alex and pressed several buttons.

"I just made an adjustment to your MeChip."

"It seems the same," Alex observed. "Everything still looks better than it really is."

"Yes. I've only turned off the internal microphone, which means it cannot eavesdrop on our conversation."

"Okay," Alex nodded. "What about the tracking device?"

"That's a little more difficult. I'm not going to try turning that off just yet."

"But won't they be able to find me?"

"If they're actively looking for you, yes. But that's a risk we'll need to take. Follow me, please."

"Where are we going?" Alex asked as Locke led them into another garden.

"The houses on this side of the alley lead to Oak Street. And I happen to know that this particular house is empty during the day. I can even get us in. Look." He stopped by a small, plastic garden gnome, stooped down, lifted it, and started fishing around with his fingers in the dirt. A moment later he held up an old-fashioned brass key.

"How did you know it was there?" Alex asked, surprised, as his mentor unlocked the back door and led them through the house. "By spying on my neighbors," he smiled, a mischievous glint in his eyes. "It always pays to have an escape route planned, Alex."

A millisec later and they were at the front door. Locke pulled it open and scanned the street. So far, there was no sign of the Regs. Locke led them outside, looked up and down the street again, and crossed it. There was a car parked on the other side. The old man pulled out some keys and pressed a button. The doors unlocked with a loud click.

"Get in."

Once inside, Locke turned the key in the ignition and the engine sputtered into life. A moment later and they had pulled away.

They were already several blocks from Larchmont Street when the sirens sounded and a Reg patrol car came tearing towards them from the opposite direction, overtaking another vehicle and entering their lane. For a millisec, Alex thought it was going to screech to a halt in front of them and block their path, but instead it swerved back onto the right side of the street and accelerated away.

"That was close," Alex said, exhaling.

"Very," Locke agreed.

"Where are we going?" Alex asked.

"You'll know soon enough," Locke replied, evidently concentrating on his driving.

"Shouldn't we be going a bit faster?"

"Only if we want to draw attention to ourselves," Locke answered, his eyes still on the road. "To escape detection we need to blend in, go with the flow of traffic."

"Can I ask you something?" Alex said after a short silence.

"Let us get to our destination, then all will be revealed," Locke replied.

This was easier said than done. Alex was bursting with questions. After a few more minutes, he couldn't hold it in any longer: "Can't you at least tell me who was sending me those messages?" he asked at last.

"I can do better than that. I can introduce you to them," Locke replied. As he spoke, he pulled the car into a driveway next to what looked to Alex like a disused auto repair shop. A garage door opened automatically and Locke drove slowly inside. Behind them, Alex heard the door begin to shut, its electric motor making the familiar grinding sound.

Locke led them out of the garage and down a corridor which ended in another door.

"This way," Locke said, opening the door and motioning for Alex to enter first.

The large room was dimly lit, with just one bulb hanging from the middle of the ceiling, but Alex saw at once that his hunch about a car repair establishment had been right. There were a couple of vehicle lifts on one side, benches with screwdrivers, wrenches, socket sets, clamps, and all sorts of other gear. A minivan was parked by the doors. The odor of oil was all around.

As his eyes adjusted to the light, Alex saw the figure. He was standing at a high desk staring at a computer screen, his back to them, shrouded in shadow.

"We're here," Locke announced.

The person turned and grunted in recognition. He advanced towards them, finally stepping into the circle of light.

"Welcome," he said in a voice Alex knew all too well.

19 | The Enemy

The man was stocky and powerfully built, dressed in a dark greatcoat. His hair was cut short, brown but flecked throughout with gray. His face was impassive as he looked at Alex with those hooded blue eyes Alex now knew all too well.

"What the smeck is *he* doing here?" Alex said, tearing his eyes away from the figure in front of him and turning to his mentor at last.

"He's here to help," John Locke replied calmly. "He has decided to join our revolution."

"And you actually believe him?" Alex asked, staring at Locke incredulously. "Surely you can't believe him?"

"Actually, I do."

Alex looked from one to the other in astonishment.

"But he's a murderer," Alex said at last.

"Probably," Locke replied.

"And he betrayed you."

"Definitely."

"Then how can you possibly think he's on our side?" Alex insisted, his voice rising as he looked back at Locke's nemesis, at the traitor who'd done more than anyone to maintain the MeChip's evil grip on the country for more than 15 years: General Slade Arnold.

"Explain it to me again," Alex said a few minutes later. He was in control of himself now, his anger subsiding as he had listened to Arnold's explanation and Locke's reassurances. But he still felt on edge,

79

tense and uncertain as he looked at the man who'd caused so much suffering.

"As I said already, I have seen the error of my ways," Arnold repeated, his voice smooth and soft, his accent still elusive: American mostly, but with a hint of something else. Was it Australian, perhaps? Or English?

"Seeing my son Iggy after so many years reminded me of what I have lost; what I gave up for power," Arnold continued. "And in recent years President Davison has become more erratic, vengeful, and dangerous. I am afraid she may harm Iggy and his mother. I can no longer predict what the President will do next."

"So you joined us because you're afraid of her and worried about your family?"

"Yes, but it's more—"

"I am sorry to interrupt, Slade, but providing a more detailed explanation to Alex must wait for another time," John Locke said firmly. "We need to turn our attention back to our present dilemma. Somehow the Regs found out where I was hiding. Do you have any idea why?"

"No," Slade Arnold replied, grimacing. "In the past such orders would have come through me, but Davora—the President I mean—recently put Charles Tarleton in charge of the Regulators."

"Tarleton?" Locke asked.

"Colonel Tarleton—or I should say, General Tarleton after his recent promotion—is one of the President's aides in the White House. He's an untrustworthy, backstabbing—"

"Takes one to know one," Alex interrupted. "And speaking of trust, I still don't believe you're on our side."

"But I do," Locke insisted. "And right now we are running out of time."

"Time for what?" Alex asked.

"Time to extract others who are at risk of being arrested by the Regs."

"Like who?"

"Anyone connected with our adventures in the forest may be in danger: your parents, for a start; Abby and her family; your friends Sol, Tom, and Harriet; possibly their parents, too; and Iggy and Alice Elgar, of course," Locke said, looking at Arnold as he spoke those last two names.

"What do we do?" Alex asked.

"We already have a plan to take them somewhere safe," Locke said.

"Yes, but we did not expect to have to implement it so soon. Not everyone who would help with the extraction is in position," Arnold said.

"Who's missing?" Locke asked.

"Nelly isn't here with her team yet; she's in D.C. And Sybil and Electa are still on another mission."

"Wait, what? Are you saying Sybil and Electa are alive?" Alex asked, wonder and relief flooding through him in equal measure.

"Yes, and they have been playing an important part in our rebellion. But we have no time for that now."

"But—"

"Alex, your questions must wait!" Locke repeated firmly. "So Slade, who is available?"

"Captain Bailey is here with five of her team."

"Captain Bailey?" Alex began, but stopped at a quelling look from Locke.

"If they split up into three groups of two, we could have them liberate Sol, Tom, Harriet, and their families," Arnold continued.

"That would spread us very thin," Locke observed. "If the Regs intervene, we'd probably be outnumbered."

"True. But I don't see any other way, do you?" General Arnold responded.

"No," Locke admitted, shaking his head. "And you'll get Iggy and Alice, I presume?" the old man asked Arnold, who nodded.

"That just leaves your parents, Alex, plus Abby and her folks next door."

"Who'll save them?" Alex asked his mentor.

"Since you and I are the only other members of the team here in Lincoln, Alex, I think it will have to be us."

20 | Rage

"Was it Arnold sending me those MeChip messages?" Alex asked as he sat next to Locke in the old minivan Slade Arnold had given them.

"He masterminded it, yes. But we're not doing this alone, Alex. There are others all around the country who are a part of the revolution now, and more are joining each day," Locke assured him, taking his eyes off the road for a millisec to look at his young companion.

"But why were the messages—the clues—so difficult to figure out?"

"We were trying to minimize our use of the MeChip so it would be hard for our enemies to trace. That is why we only sent the first full message via MeChip. The other clues were all left on street corners.

"Then how did they find your hideout?"

"I wish I knew," Locke answered, frowning. "How's your wrist, by the way?"

"It's fine. I mean, it hurts but it's not broken. Just burned."

"You were lucky it was nothing worse. You did well to defeat those Regs."

"It wasn't so hard now I can control people's MeChips."

"Your control is very impressive, Alex, although I hope you understand why I will have to disable your MeChip completely once we free your parents. We cannot afford to be tracked down by the Fixers again."

"But I thought General Arnold was still in charge of the Fixers? Aren't they the ones who find people through their MeChips?"

"Yes, the Fixers are constantly looking for signs of unusual behavior, and they are assisted by sophisticated AI systems."

"So why doesn't Arnold tell them to stop searching here in Lincoln?"

"It would appear too suspicious. Besides, others in government have that authority, too. Better to be safe than sorry. We will turn off your MeChip once we have your parents and Abby's family with us."

"John ... how did you get out of prison?"

"That was also Arnold's doing. It wasn't easy, and we had quite an adventure of it, but he managed it. I have a lot to thank him for lately."

"He'll never make up for what he's done in the past," Alex declared bitterly.

"He's certainly trying."

"I still don't trust him."

"I don't blame you, Alex. But I believe he's sincere. I believe seeing Iggy in such danger during our battle in Hope, and then seeing Alice again, rekindled something inside him. Almost there," Locke said as he turned the corner onto Alex's street, now illuminated in the gathering dusk by the vehicle's powerful headlamps.

"You remember the plan?"

"Yes. You fetch Abby and her parents while I use my MeChip control to convince my parents to join us. We get back in the car and rendezvous with Arnold. Simple."

"Exactly. And don't forget—"

But Locke suddenly stopped speaking. Jerking the steering wheel and slamming on the brakes, he pulled over to the side of the road. Parked in front of Alex's house were two large black vans. Their back doors were open and about a dozen Regs were clambering out, weapons ready. One of the Regs spotted their minivan and began striding towards them, while the others fanned out in the opposite direction, heading towards Alex and Abby's homes.

The Reg stopped about 30 yards away from the vehicle.

"Stay in the car. Let me handle this," Locke said, pushing open the door and taking a step towards the man.

"Don't move!" the Reg commanded, pointing his weapon at Locke.

"It's fine, officer," Locke said, taking another step forward.

"I said don't move. I'm checking your vehicle."

"Very well," Locke replied, still inching forward.

What was Locke doing, Alex wondered? Then he realized. His remote control only worked over a short distance. He must be trying to get in range. But what if it didn't work?

"My records show this vehicle is stolen," the Reg declared. "Stay where you are and place your hands above your head. I said stay where you are!" he shouted, for Locke had taken another step towards him.

"Hey, what's that in your hand?"

"It's nothing, officer, I—"

Fzzoom!

The laser beam struck Locke in his chest. He fell backwards, landing on his back on the hard asphalt. His eyes were closed. The Reg approached cautiously, weapon in hand, still pointing it at Locke. Then the man saw Alex.

"You. Get out of the vehicle. Now!"

But Alex didn't move. The man was closer now, close enough for Alex's power to reach him, for the tendrils of light to stretch from Alex's brain to his foe's MeChip, to implant any idea he wished. And Alex was angry. Beyond angry.

The Reg's eyes grew wide as Alex's attack struck him. He dropped his weapon and sank to the ground, his hands tearing at his hair. Alex opened the car door and strode purposefully towards his enemy. Picking the gun up from the ground, Alex raised it and shot the man in the side of the head.

At such close range, the blast smashed him to the ground. His peaked cap, which now had white smoke rising from it, remained on his head but was askew, partly concealing his face. The silver eagle button that adorned every Reg's cap had snapped off and lay in the gutter, glinting in the streetlamp's dim glow.

As quickly as it had arrived, Alex's rage—the *madness* that had gripped him at seeing Locke shot—washed away from him like water down a drain. He looked down at the gun in his hands and breathed a sigh of relief as he saw the setting.

Stun. Not kill. So he was not a murderer. The Reg was alive. And that meant Locke was, too. Hastening over to the old man, Alex leaned over him, checking for signs of life. Leaning in and straining to hear, he caught the sound of shallow breathing.

Alex dragged Locke off the road and lay him gently on the sidewalk next to the minivan, before taking the remote control from the insensible old man.

This was all he could do for him for the time being, Alex realized. He was needed elsewhere.

Alex stood up. Gun in one hand, remote in the other, he strode towards his house.

21 | Set to Kill

Alex's front door was open wide as he approached, weapons at the ready. He stopped at the entrance and listened. For a millisec there was silence. Then a voice rang out.

"Why are you doing this, officer? We haven't done anything wrong."

It was his mom. A moment later, his dad—or more accurately, the man who thought he was Alex's dad—spoke:

"Hey, take your hands off her!"

There were sounds of hasty movement, the scraping of a chair on the linoleum, a loud banging sound, and a groan.

Alex rushed down the hallway, stopping at the open kitchen door.

Three Regs had Alex's dad pinned. He was still standing but was leaning forward, his face pressed against the kitchen table as two of the Regs held him down and a third tried to put handcuffs on his wrists, which were pulled up behind his back. Two more Regs were restraining his mom, who was struggling unsuccessfully against them.

Alex pointed Locke's remote control and pressed a button. Instantly, the three Regs who were attacking his dad froze. Their hands dropped placidly by their sides, their mouths fell open slightly and their eyes became glassy and unfocused. The other two Regs saw Alex. One stepped away from his mom and pulled out his weapon, as Alex pressed the remote again.

Nothing happened. The man drew his gun and Alex raised his. Both fired at the same time, Alex diving to his left as he pulled the trigger.

His shot struck the man in the chest and he collapsed instantly to the floor, while the Reg's blast struck the door exactly at the spot Alex had been standing just a millisec earlier.

Alex, now on his knees, pointed his weapon at the other Reg. But he didn't shoot. The man was using his mom as a shield, one arm wrapped around her neck, his laz-pistol pointing at the side of her head.

"Drop your weapon or she gets it," the Reg ordered.

Alex stood there unmoving, unsure what to do.

"I mean it. My weapon's set to kill. Now drop it!"

Alex lowered his weapon and set it on the ground.

"You, go join the boy," the Reg said, directing his instructions at Alex's dad, who stepped back from the three frozen Regs.

"What have you done to the others? Why are they—" the Reg began, his eyes flitting between Alex and his comrades. Then he stopped. His eyes widened in horror as he stared off to his right. Forgetting all about Alex's mom, who stumbled away from him, he pointed his weapon at the fridge.

"Get back. I mean it! Get back!" the Reg ordered, still staring at the imaginary monster Alex had implanted in his mind through his MeChip. Casually, Alex leaned down, picked up the laz-pistol, and shot the Reg in the stomach. He slumped to the ground, unconscious. Meanwhile, the other three Regs continued to stare abstractedly at the ground, either unaware of, or uninterested in, the matters of life-and-death going on around them.

Alex's mom staggered over to his dad, who embraced her. The two of them turned to Alex.

"What's going on, Alex? What's happening?"

"It's okay. Trust me. I know what to do."

"But the Regs just attacked us for no reason. Who can help us? Should I call the army? The State Guard?" his dad asked.

Once more, Alex used his MeChip, reaching out to theirs to help calm them.

Trust me. All will be well. Trust me and do exactly as I say.

Alex saw his parents exhale, the looks of panic fade just a little.

"Leave now and find a white minivan. It's down the street in the direction of Mr. Jay's house. There's an old man lying on the sidewalk. He's a friend and he has the keys. See if you can wake him. If you can't, put him safely in the minivan. Wait for me there. I'll be along soon. Okay?"

His parents nodded and set off down the hallway. A moment later and they had left the house.

Alex took a deep breath. He looked at the three frozen Regs. How long would they stay incapacitated? Had Locke ever told him? If so, he couldn't recall. Hoping it would be long enough for what he had to do, he disarmed all of them, taking their weapons and setting them on the table.

The Reg had been telling the truth, Alex realized in alarm as he looked at them. They were all now set to kill, not stun. Hurriedly, Alex picked up the guns and made his way back into the hallway. Opening a closet, his stuffed the weapons behind several pairs of old boots and shoes, keeping just one for himself. Laz-pistol in one hand, remote control in the other, he stepped carefully out the front door.

It was almost fully dark now as the last rays of light stretched out from behind the far-off mountains and the pinkish hues of evening sky faded into navy blues and grays. Checking one more time that his laz-pistol was set to stun rather than kill, he advanced across his garden, vaulted the fence, and crept towards Abby's house.

The front door was open, but this one looked as though it had been forced. Two of the panes of glass had been smashed and the whole structure was askew, hanging off one of its hinges.

He was just about to step over the threshold when there was a succession of sounds from within:

Bang! Fzzoom! Bang! Fzzoom! Fzzoom! Fzzoom!

Two voices screamed; a man's, then a woman's. Alex rushed forward, heedless of the risk. At the end of the hallway he saw four Regs sheltering behind a table and some chairs. Two more were lying on the ground, blood coursing from wounds to stomach and chest. The four uninjured Regs were facing away from Alex, firing repeatedly up a flight of stairs. As they blazed away, there was a groan from up above and a figure came tumbling down the steps. The stairwell was unlit and Alex couldn't tell in the semi-darkness who it was. But he knew it could only be Abby or one of her parents.

Again, Alex tried the remote control. This time, two of the Regs froze, their arms falling to their sides, heads lowered, weapons slipping from their grasp. Before the other two even knew what was happening, Alex had stunned them with his laz-pistol and they were both out cold on the kitchen floor.

Alex rushed forward. Lying at the foot of the steps was the man Abby thought of as her father. His eyes were open but there was no life in them. Thin trails of blood were stealing from his nose and mouth. His limbs were splayed out at odd angles. An old rifle was still clutched in one hand.

There was a sound on the landing above and a moment later Abby came rushing down, taking the steps two at a time. She pulled up short as she saw the fallen figure of her father. Her mother brushed past her and fell upon his body, pulling him towards her.

"Ohmygod, ohmygod, don't be dead, don't be dead, don't be dead," she pleaded repeatedly as Abby looked on, seemingly rooted to the spot, her eyes wide.

Abby's mother looked up at her daughter. Their eyes met ... and Abby cracked, dropping to her knees and embracing her, the tears finally falling. Alex looked away, embarrassed at witnessing their private grief. He wanted to leave them alone, to let them feel their sorrow. But he knew they had to leave; to get out of there urgently.

"I'm so sorry, so very sorry for your loss. But we have to go right now," he said at last.

"What?" Abby asked, looking up as if noticing him for the first time. "We're not leaving, Alex. We need to call for help, to ... to get these evil people arrested."

"We can't," Alex said. "Please trust me. We must go right away."

"What are you talking about?" Abby asked, her voice cracking as her mom wrapped her arms around her dead husband once more, rocking back and forth.

"We need to go," Alex repeated gently. "We're not safe here." But Abby had already turned back to her parents, Alex apparently forgotten.

What could he do? Feeling oddly guilty at intruding on their grief, Alex reached out with his MeChip:

You must leave here now. Trust Alex. He will take you to safety. Do as Alex asks.

Slowly, mother and daughter raised their eyes and looked at him.

"Please come with me," he said. "I'll take you to safety." After a moment's hesitation, Abby nodded. With their arms around one another's shoulders and several backward glances, they followed him through the kitchen where he quickly disarmed all the Regs, shoving their weapons deep into a closet like he'd done at his own home. For good measure, he added the laz-pistol he'd been using to the pile of hidden weapons.

"We're going to join my parents and escape," he said, turning to Abby and her mom.

"But what—"

"I'll explain everything later. Follow me, please. This way," he instructed, his heart breaking for the two sobbing figures as he led them away from their home and out into the night.

22 | Leaving Lincoln

"**I**s he awake?" Alex asked his mom, who was standing by the minivan.

"Yes, although he seems pretty shaken up. He's in the passenger seat. Your dad's going to drive. Susanna, why are you and Abby here? And where's John?" Alex's mom asked as her neighbors emerged into the light of the streetlamp.

"We'll explain in the car. Come on, we have to go," Alex said, urging them into the vehicle and looking anxiously over his shoulder for signs of pursuit as Susanna started sobbing once more.

"Where to?" Alex's dad asked as soon as the doors were closed.

"Lincoln High, please," Locke muttered from the seat beside him, slurring slightly as he spoke.

They arrived a few minutes later. Alex's dad pulled into the car park and drew to a halt.

"What now?" Alex's dad enquired.

Locke didn't reply straight away. Instead, he pulled out the remote control, pointed it at each of them in turn, and pressed several buttons.

"What's happened?" Alex's mom asked, looking around her. "Things look different, somehow. And something's wrong with my MeChip."

"I have disabled it. None of them should be working now."

"Why?"

"That will take a little while to explain. In the meantime, to be safe we should remove them completely."

"But why?" Alex's mom persisted.

"I will explain soon. For now, I ask you to trust me. Alex, will you help?"

Together they removed everyone's MeChips. Abby helped take out Alex's, leaving him feeling strangely vulnerable and exposed. With a pang, he realized his special powers were now gone.

When he had gathered everyone's MeChips, Locke stepped out of the car, dropped them on the concrete, and ground them underfoot.

"Is he alright?" Alex's dad enquired in an undertone as they watched Locke from inside the car. "Am I the only one who thinks destroying our MeChips is weird?"

"He's doing the right thing," Alex tried to reassure them. "He's just trying to keep us safe. He'll explain everything soon."

"Something's wrong," Abby said in alarm, her eyes darting left and right. "I know it's dark, but something looks different about the car. And outside, too."

"Yes," Alex agreed, "but it'll be okay. I promise."

Locke opened the passenger door and poked his head back inside the vehicle.

"Now that's done we need to get back on the road. Ben, I'll take over the driving, if you don't mind."

"Are you feeling up to it?" Alex asked, concerned.

"I'll manage," Locke replied as the two men exchanged seats.

Locke turned the key in the ignition and pulled out of the school parking lot.

"So what's going on? Can someone please talk to me? I need to know I'm not going crazy," Alex's mom said, her voice shaking slightly.

"Alex, will you tell them? I should concentrate on my driving," Locke replied.

Alex spoke for a long time. The group listened in silence, the only interruption coming from Susanna's occasional sobs. He spoke to them about what he'd learned from Locke about the plot years before to control people through their MeChips, fast-forwarding to what had happened in recent months: the Best Band contest, their adventures in the forest, the battle for Hope, and their recapture and return to Lincoln.

They had been driving for more than an hour by the time Alex reached the point in the story where he'd recently regained his memories. Locke had driven them out of Lincoln and onto the freeway heading south, taking them along a highway traversing forested hills. The road seemed to be little used, with only the occasional car or truck heading in the other direction. So far, there was no sign of pursuit.

Alex was about to explain what he'd done after regaining his memory when Abby interrupted.

"Why can't I remember any of this?"

"You will," Alex answered. "Now your MeChip's removed it'll come back little by little, like it did before. It just takes time. Eventually, you'll know everything—far more than I've told you, even."

Alex stole a glance at her as he said this. He was feeling guilty at what he'd already omitted from his story. He hadn't, for instance, mentioned how both their real fathers had died some time ago. The man Abby thought was her dad—but who was in fact a replacement—had just been shot to death in front of her, while the man who believed he was Alex's father was sitting with them in the car. How could he try to explain this just now? Surely it was not the time for such revelations—not on top of everything else he'd just told them. Belatedly, Alex could appreciate now why Locke had withheld information from them when they had been regaining their memories for the first time during their trek through the forest. Had his mentor felt there was too much to burden people with in one go?

"You were about to tell us what happened once you regained your memories, Alex," his mom prompted him after a lengthy silence.

"Yes. Sorry. So, I ... um ... came up with a plan. First, I learned to control my own MeChip, then ... hey, where are we going?" Alex asked, for Locke was taking the minivan onto an offramp and leaving the freeway.

"We're heading to our first meeting point," Locke replied, his eyes still on the darkened road.

23 | The Cabin

The road soon narrowed into a single lane. The asphalt was cracked and uneven, making the minivan bump and shake. The trees gradually drew closer on either side, with branches snaking overhead and blocking out the night sky. There were no streetlamps and the only source of illumination was the car headlights, which sliced two narrow beams of brightness into the dark pressing in from all sides. They drove in silence for about ten minutes before emerging into a clearing. It was the size of a football field and bounded by trees. Alex breathed a sigh of relief as he saw the sky and stars once more. Without them, and with the forest hemming them in, he'd felt like they'd been driving in a tunnel underground. It was a sensation that left him feeling queasy.

At first, Alex thought the clearing was empty. But as they approached the far side the dark outline of a building came into view, just off to the right of the road. Locke pulled into the driveway and stopped the car. For a moment, the headlights illuminated the structure; it was a large, log cabin the size of a house.

"It seems we're the first to arrive," he muttered to himself.

"Is this the meeting point?" Abby asked.

"Yes, but not our final destination. Follow me, please." Locke led them up several steps on to a porch, stopping in front of the door.

"Do you have the key?" Alex's mom asked.

"No, but there's a keypad. Just a moment." A millisec later and there was a loud click as the door unlocked. "Wait for me here. I'll be back in a moment."

There was the sound of movement from within but it was hard to make out what Locke was doing in the shadows. After a few seconds, a light flicked on, then a second, illuminating two small circles of space. Locke stepped back into view, holding two battery-powered lanterns.

"Take this and make yourselves at home," Locke said, handing one of the lamps to Alex's dad. "I have to turn on the generator that powers the building. Abby, will you help me?"

Locke and Abby disappeared around the side of the porch, while the rest of them filed inside. In the dull light of the lantern, Alex saw a large living room with a couch, several chairs, and a fireplace. The group sat down and waited.

From outside, Alex heard a loud clicking sound followed by a steady whirring drone.

"What's that?" Alex asked.

"Probably a diesel generator," his mom replied. "The electricity should come on soon." There were footsteps by the door, then an overhead electric light turned on illuminating the room much more brightly. Locke was by the entrance once more, his finger on the light switch. Abby was just behind him.

"First things first, I need to let our friends know we're here. Alex, will you join me?" Locke led Alex through a doorway and down a corridor with doors leading off to left and right. At the end of the corridor was another locked door with a keypad. Again, Locke entered the right digits and led them inside a small, windowless room.

It was simply furnished, with an old wooden desk and two chairs. On the desk stood a small silver and black box with knobs and buttons on the front. A coiled cable led from the back of the device into a small black piece of plastic about the size of a person's palm.

"What's that?" Alex asked.

"A radio transmitter." Locke sat down, pressed a couple of buttons on the device, then picked up the piece of plastic and spoke into it: "This is DJL to base, DJL to base ... do you copy?"

There was a buzz of static, followed by silence.

"DJL to base. Do you copy?" Locke repeated.

It seemed to Alex that no one was out there. They waited for at least thirty seconds before the silence was finally broken and a voice came crackling out of the device, indistinct and faint. Locke raised the volume and turned one of the knobs, seeking a better signal. After several attempts, the words became suddenly clear and distinct:

"I repeat, this is base. This is base. What is your location?"

"We're at LC One."

"LC One, copy. How many?"

"Six, but we expect more soon."

"Copy that. An extraction team will arrive tomorrow at 0800. Are you secure until then?"

"I think so."

"Injuries?"

"None so far."

"Good. Expect the team in the morning. Over and out."

Locke turned off the device and returned to the living room.

"Any news?" Alex's mom asked.

"Yes, our friends will collect us in the morning."

"What happens now?" Abby asked.

"Now we have a late supper and a warm drink. Then we sleep. This cabin has several bedrooms, each with two or three bunk beds. Plenty of room for all of us."

"Will you finish your story, Alex?" Abby asked after they had finished their simple meal of heated canned soup and started on some hot chocolate. "What happened once you regained your memories?"

Alex continued his tale as they sat around the kitchen table, holding his steaming mug in both hands. He told the truth as far as he could, only omitting embarrassing details like using his new powers to get revenge on Iggy and his buddy Eric. Finally, he described what had happened earlier that day, including his reunion with John Locke, meeting General Arnold, and their decision to try to liberate Sol, Tom, Harriet, Iggy, and their families in case the Regs tried to arrest them.

"A very smart decision, given what happened to us," Alex's dad observed.

"But where are they?" Abby asked. "Shouldn't they be here by now?"

As if on cue, a light lanced through the window. Alex and Abby jumped up and peered outside. "It's a car," Abby said a moment later. "What should we do?"

"Hope for the best and prepare for the worst," Locke replied, rising to his feet and pulling three remote controls from his pockets. "Alex, can you please explain to Abby how they work? Then hide somewhere out of sight, but be ready to use your weapons. Ben, Liz, Susanna, you will find several old guns and ammunition down the corridor, last door on the right."

"What will you do?" Alex asked.

"Why, greet our guests, of course," Locke replied, walking briskly towards the porch.

Alex quickly explained to Abby how to use the remote controls to immobilize anyone with a MeChip. They then hid behind one of the couches after turning off the living room light.

A minute later, however, the light was back on.

"It's alright, you can come out," Locke announced.

Alex and Abby stood up while their parents emerged from the corridor, each holding an old-fashioned pistol.

Alice and Iggy Elgar entered the room, followed a moment later by General Slade Arnold. Alex and Abby's moms both stepped forward and hugged Alice.

"Nice to see you, Abby," Iggy said, smiling at her while ignoring Alex.

"Where are the others?" Slade Arnold asked, turning to Locke.

"They haven't arrived yet."

"That's not good." Arnold shook his head. "How did your extraction go?"

"Badly. The Regs were already there and we ... we lost Alice's husband John," Locke said, his voice dropping to a whisper. "How about you?"

"Similar," Arnold replied, his eyes flicking briefly towards Alice and Abby. "The Regs' weapons were all set to kill, which is a serious change of protocol. Can we step outside? We need to talk."

Slade Arnold and Locke moved onto the porch, speaking briefly in hushed tones before returning to the group.

"We've decided General Arnold and I will wait up for the others to arrive. The rest of you should get some sleep," Locke declared.

"That doesn't sound fair," Alex's mom chimed in. "Besides, we're depending on the two of you to make your plan work properly. We need you both well rested and in good shape for whatever comes next."

Locke and Arnold tried to argue, but most of the others insisted on sharing the burden. "We'll take it in shifts while you sleep," Alex said, finally joining the conversation.

"I'll go first, then my mom, then my ... um ... dad, then Iggy, then Alice," Alex said, thinking that Abby and Susanna shouldn't be asked to join in given what had just happened to them.

"I want to do my share," Abby said fiercely.

"Good, then you can take my turn," Iggy interrupted, yawning loudly. "I'm beat." And with that, he headed down the corridor to one of the bedrooms before anyone could argue.

"I must admit, I could use some sleep," Locke relented at last. "How about you, Slade?"

"Fine," General Arnold said. "I just need to speak with our allies on the radio and then I'll turn in."

The others all headed towards the bedrooms, leaving Alex alone in the main room. He turned off the light and sat in the semi-darkness, his eyes fixed on the windows for sights or sounds of a vehicle.

Nothing. Where were the others? Had they been caught? Or worse? With an effort, he forced himself to think about something else. His mind wandered over the day's events. Was it really just a few hours ago that he'd finally found Locke? And what about Slade Arnold? Was he actually on their side? An old grandfather clock in the corner finally struck one in the morning as Alex stifled a yawn. Time to wake up his mom so she could take the next shift.

He was just about to fetch her when something outside caught his attention. He rushed to the door, opened it, and looked out. Heading towards the house were two vehicles, one in front of the other, their lights rising and falling over the rough ground.

24 | Cabin Fever

The two automobiles pulled up next to the minivan and Arnold's car. Alex sighed in relief as he saw Tom in the passenger seat of one. A millisec later and Sol had emerged from the other. He saw Alex.

"We need help."

Alex rushed down the stairs just as Sol started pulling his father out of the car. The man looked unsteady on his feet and his head was wrapped in a makeshift bandage. A woman emerged from the driver's side: Captain Bailey, the leader of Hope's militia.

"Where are your medical supplies?" she asked, instantly taking charge of the situation.

"Wait here. I'll get help." Alex rushed off and gently woke Locke, who grabbed the first aid kit from the bathroom. Moving quietly and closing the door to the corridor so as not to wake the others, Locke followed Alex outside and together they helped the new arrivals into the main room. It was not a pretty sight.

Tom's mom had burn marks on her legs and was barely able to walk. His father had a bandaged, blood-stained arm and seemed to have a fever, sweat dripping from his face. Tom himself had a black eye and busted lip, while Sol's mom and dad both had head injuries. Captain Bailey had an angry-looking welt on her neck. Only Sol and the single soldier from Captain Bailey's team who had arrived with Tom appeared uninjured.

Locke, Alex, Sol, and the soldier immediately began tending to the injured, cleaning wounds and fixing bandages as best they could.

"Where are your other troops?" Locke asked Captain Bailey as he cleaned her injured neck. "I thought there would be four of you?"

"Lynn and Dave didn't make it," Captain Bailey replied, staring at the ground.

"I'm very sorry," Locke said softly.

"Who else is here? Did the others all arrive?" Sol asked, looking from Locke to Alex.

"Everyone's here except Harriet and her family," Alex replied.

Sol just stared at Alex, a look of shock on his face.

"Harriet's ... not here?" he asked at last, as if unable to believe what he was hearing.

"Not yet," Alex replied.

There was another lengthy silence. Tom got up and put a hand on his friend's shoulder.

"It'll be okay, Sol. She'll get here, I just know it." But Sol didn't respond. He just stood there, staring out the window in a daze.

Finally, when they had treated everyone's injuries, Locke spoke again.

"Time for you all to get some sleep. Please use the first two doors on the left; those rooms are unoccupied and have bunk beds. Since I'm awake I'll take the next shift and wait up for the last group to arrive."

"No," Sol said, his voice no longer its typical calm monotone, but fierce and insistent. "I'll wait up. I want to be awake when they get here."

They had still not arrived by the time Alex woke the next morning. He wandered into the main room to find Sol arguing with his, Alex's, mom.

"I told you, Liz," Sol said, "I wanted to be here when they arrived."

"But you should have woken me, Sol. You look exhausted."

"I'm fine," Sol replied dismissively.

But he wasn't. His eyes were bloodshot and half-closed. He looked utterly spent.

"Any news?" Locke asked as he entered the room a moment later, stifling a yawn.

"Nothing," Sol replied, not meeting Locke's gaze.

Locke frowned as he glanced at the grandfather clock.

"It's almost 7. We should wake the others."

An hour later and the group was almost done cleaning the dishes after a breakfast of hot oatmeal and coffee. There had been little conversation—everyone seemed too stunned by recent events—although there were several sidelong glances at Slade Arnold, who seemed out-of-place among the group. Alex was just putting the last of the dishes away when there was a noise from outside.

"That's them. It has to be them!" Sol declared, his expression lifting as he rushed out of the kitchen and pulled open the front door, followed a moment later by Tom and the others.

But it wasn't Harriet and her family. As Alex joined his friends on the porch, the sound came more clearly over the humming of the generator.

Alex scanned the forest road but saw nothing. No cars, no trucks, nothing at all. Then something caught his attention from a different direction. Shielding his eyes against the sun, he looked up above the tree line to his right.

Whup-whup-whup-whup.

It was a helicopter. And it was heading directly towards them.

25 | The Base

Who was in the helicopter? Was it the enemy? Tom seemed in no doubt. He sprinted back into the house and emerged seconds later with a rifle, which he aimed up into the sky in the direction of the approaching machine.

"Put that down, boy," General Arnold grunted. "You might hurt yourself. They're our allies."

"Is he telling the truth, Dr. L?" Tom asked uncertainly, turning to Locke for confirmation.

"You've remembered your nickname for me," John Locke said, smiling. "And yes, I believe he is. I am expecting our friends to arrive at 8 a.m."

"Unless the Regs intercepted the message," Iggy interjected.

"A fair point, Iggy. There's no harm in being cautious. Thomas, Sol, Abby, Alex, and Iggy, why don't you take up positions nearby in the forest? If there's trouble you can come to our aid," Locke suggested, his eyes still on the chopper.

The five of them retreated into the house, grabbed more weapons, and emerged through a back door into the forest, where they concealed themselves behind nearby trees. Alex peered through the foliage as the helicopter approached, hovering above the ground about fifty yards away from the cabin. It touched down and the rotor blades began to slow.

Several figures emerged. They were dressed in military fatigues but only two held weapons. Two more were carrying a big black box between them. Iggy lifted his rifle and aimed, but Alex raised a hand to stop him.

"Wait up. I think they're medics."

The figures approached the cabin and Alex noticed a red cross on a white background emblazoned on top of the box. Locke and Arnold stepped forward and Alex could hear them exchange greetings with the newcomers, although he couldn't make out more than a few words. A moment later, Locke turned in their direction and raised his voice.

"You can come out. These are the friends we were expecting."

Alex clutched the sides of his seat as the helicopter banked to one side. His stomach lurched as it started to descend. Was it supposed to be doing this or were they plunging to their doom? He looked at the others sitting across the aisle in the seats opposite his. Tom had turned pale and his eyes were shut. He'd probably never flown before, either, Alex decided. But Locke and Arnold looked calm, as if this was perfectly normal. Alex would have asked them, but the noise of the rotor blades was loud and unrelenting, preventing easy conversation.

Alex's ears popped as they continued to descend. Taking his cue from Locke, Alex tried to remain calm. This is all perfectly normal, he said to himself over and over, like a monk reciting a mantra. He wished he could see outside but there were no windows in this part of the machine; only two rows of low-slung seats facing each other and metal walls crisscrossed with silver pipes, colored cables, and wires. What were they all for, he wondered?

Alex felt the chopper pause in its descent, as if suspended in midair. Then it began inching lower again, shaking and juddering slightly before touching down with a thud. The rotors started to slow and Arnold and Locke unclipped their seatbelts and stood up. Alex and the others followed their lead. The large metal door at the rear of the vehicle lowered and Arnold hopped down, ducking his head to avoid the low metal frame. Alex and the others did the same. Squinting in the sunshine, Alex looked around.

They were by the entrance to a hangar. It was the size of a football field, with metal walls enclosing a smooth concrete floor. The high silver ceilings were intersected with pipes and girders. The helicopter had landed just inside the colossal structure. Looking outside, Alex saw a second large building connected by a covered walkway. Behind it, a long, empty airplane runway stretched away into the distance.

Inside, the hangar was a hive of activity. People were everywhere. Close by, mechanics in coveralls were working on a range of vehicles: a long row of trucks, half-a-dozen armored personnel carriers, and three tanks lined up against the nearest wall. Next to their helicopter were several more choppers, as well as two military jet aircraft, the insignia of the U.S. Air Force emblazoned on their sides. Two young women were driving forklifts back and forth as they shifted large crates.

Towards the far wall were several rows of computers, dozens in all. In front of each, a techie sat peering intently at a screen, occasionally manipulating an old-fashioned mouse or typing something rapidly onto an ancient keyboard.

Armed guards were everywhere, some standing in position, their eyes flicking back and forth, others hurrying around on important business, weapons holstered or slung over shoulders.

But General Arnold paid scant attention to any of this. Motioning with his hand for them to follow, he led the way quickly through the hangar towards a far door, striding down a corridor and into another building. After several minutes, they found themselves in a medical facility where they were greeted by several nurses and doctors.

"Why are we here? The medics already saw us at the cabin," Iggy said.

"That was a preliminary check-up. We need everyone to have a full examination, especially those who sustained head wounds," Arnold answered, his eyes flicking towards Sol's parents.

The medical staff took their time but finally everyone was given the all-clear.

"Now you should rest. John and I will debrief our allies while you settle in to your new quarters."

As if on cue a soldier entered, three chevrons on the shoulder of his uniform. Seeing Arnold, he snapped to attention and gave a smart salute before speaking.

"Here to escort the new arrivals to their quarters, General."

"Good," Arnold replied, before turning back to the group. "I expect an all-hands meeting later, so I'd strongly advise you to get some rest," he said, before turning to speak with Locke.

The sergeant led the rest of them out of the medical facility, down a corridor, and outside under a covered walkway, passing several guards on the way. Finally, he brought them inside yet another building. The group thinned out as the sergeant indicated rooms where people would be billeted, starting with the parents. Finally, he led Sol, Tom, Alex, and Iggy into a small but clean room with two bunkbeds.

"I don't want to share with them," Iggy spat. "Is there anywhere else?"

The sergeant regarded him for several seconds before replying.

"You have one other option."

"Which is?"

"You can sleep on the runway."

Without waiting for an answer, the man turned on his heel and walked away. Alex tried not to laugh as Iggy fumed.

"This is alright, though," Tom said as he clambered into one of the upper bunks.

"It'll do," Alex replied.

"Any idea where we are?" Tom asked.

Alex shook his head, while the others didn't respond. Sol was staring into space, a frown furrowing his brow.

"You okay, man?" Alex asked, looking at his friend with concern.

"Not really," Sol replied. "What's happened to them?"

"Harriet will be okay. She's a fighter," Tom said, but his tone lacked conviction.

"Hey, is anyone else starting to remember things now their MeChips are out?" Tom asked after a short silence, evidently keen to change the subject.

"Not much," Sol said, shrugging. "I only know what that soldier, Captain Bailey, told us in the car about the MeChip being used to control us and about our adventures in Hope and stuff. But I'm not having any actual memories that are different to how they were before."

"I am," Iggy muttered, surprising them. "I've been thinking about that night when I threw up. Something weird happened and I'm sure you were involved," he said, looking accusingly at Alex.

"What makes you think that?" Alex replying, swallowing.

"I overheard the old man Locke and my fa—I mean, General Arnold—speaking about how you'd learned to control other people's MeChips. You were there when I threw up. I was about to give you a beatdown, remember? But you did do something to stop me, didn't you?"

There was a long silence before Alex finally spoke.

"Yeah, I did," he admitted at last. "I used my MeChip to make you sick. I guess I wanted payback for all the stuff you've done to me. I'm sorry."

"You're sorry?" Iggy said, taking a step forward.

"Yeah. I guess."

"You're gonna be even sorrier once I've Tysoned you."

He took another step forward and raised his fists. But before Alex could react Sol was in front of him, squaring up to Iggy.

"What are you doing? My beef's with Alex, not you," Iggy said, looking surprised.

"He apologized. Besides, you had it coming," Sol said.

"This is none of your business, dexter. Get out of my way," Iggy replied, trying to step past him. But Sol wouldn't budge.

"Give me a reason. Go on," Sol said, his eyes drilling into Iggy's, his voice carrying an angry edge Alex had never heard in it before. In fact, Sol's entire body was taut, his powerful muscles primed and ready for action.

"Jeez, what's gotten into you?" Iggy said at last, stepping back and holding up his palms in mock surrender. "I'm going to check out the cafeteria ... you guys have all gone nuts!" he said as he left the room.

"Thanks for that, Sol. But are you alright?" Alex asked as his friend continued to stand stock still in the center of the room. Alex noticed a nerve twitching under one eye, while Sol's body was still tense, almost rigid.

"What did you say?" Sol asked, shaking his head and turning to face Alex as if he'd just remembered where he was. "Am I okay? No. I guess not," he added in an undertone, staring at the doorway Iggy had just exited.

"That was awesome, Sol. But you can't let that smeckin' braggster get to you. He's not worth it," Tom said, jumping down from his bunk.

"It's not even him, it's just—"

"Harriet. We know," Tom said, patting his friend on the back. "Listen, bud, I think you should try to catch some Zs. You hardly got a wink last night."

Sol shrugged, then nodded. Without another word, he lay down on one of the lower bunks, lowered his head onto the pillow, and rolled over to face the wall.

Taking his cue from his friend, Tom did the same, pausing only to remove his shoes before clambering onto the upper bunk.

Alex watched their unmoving figures for a while. In less than a minute, Tom's regular breathing slowed. It was clear he, for one, was already out.

Stifling a yawn, Alex decided he should try to sleep, too. He may not have been up all night like Sol, but he still felt pretty beat. After the kind of day he'd had yesterday—from tracking down Locke to the run-ins with the Regs to escaping Lincoln and the late-night drama at the cabin—he clearly needed to rest and recuperate.

Alex rubbed his eyes and looked again at his injured wrist, which was still blistered from the Reg's laz-pistol. Taking off his shoes, he climbed into one of the other beds and lay his head on the pillow. At first, thoughts kept dashing through his brain one after another, like race cars rushing past the finish line in close succession. What had happened to Harriet and her parents? Could Arnold really be trusted? Would Abby recall anything about their conversations in the tree house and the forest? When would she remember the truth about her dad? And what about his own mom and the man who thought of himself as Alex's dad? The questions kept circling around and around, like the painted horses on a moving carousel, until they all melted together and he finally drifted into a troubled sleep.

26 | Awkward Reunions

"Wakey, wakey!"

Alex opened his eyes and lifted his head off the pillow. For a millisec he had no idea where he was. Then he saw the sergeant's face at the doorway and it all came flooding back.

"You guys sure needed your shuteye, huh? We're briefing in Hangar 2 in one hour. All hands. Make a left and follow the passageway. The mess hall's on the way if you're hungry." A millisec later and he was gone.

"How long have we been out?" Tom asked, sitting up and stretching.

"A few hours, maybe?" Alex guessed. "Did you catch any Zs, Sol?"

"A few," Sol replied. But Alex wasn't so sure. Sol's eyes were red-rimmed and he still looked exhausted.

"Great! I did, too," Tom declared, evidently not noticing as he sat up in bed and stretched his arms to the ceiling. "Come on, let's eat."

The mess hall was clean, the food plain but nourishing. The three friends ate their pasta in silence as a few adults came and went. In the corner of the room was an old piano. One of the nurses who'd examined them earlier was playing a tune Alex didn't recognize. It was quiet and contemplative, definitely from the Retro-Before Time.

Reflexively and without meaning to, the fingers on Alex's left hand twitched. With a pang, Alex realized how much he was missing music. He'd give almost anything to have his guitar back, practicing chords he liked, tunes he loved. Playing always calmed him when he was anxious. It helped him think. He wondered if Abby had been in here yet? She'd love that piano, for sure.

"Attention. The all-hands meeting begins in 15 minutes. Hangar 2. I repeat, all-hands in 15."

"Wow, that was loud," Tom said, rubbing his ears as he stared in annoyance at the public address system speaker on the ceiling nearby. "Should we head?"

The boys followed the nurse, who'd risen from the piano and was leaving the room. A couple of minutes later and they were in Hangar 2. Almost as large as the hangar they'd flown into, the place was already filling up.

It was an interesting crowd, Alex thought as he looked around. Many were in military uniforms, but they ranged from army to the marines, a scattering of air force, and even a few navy personnel. Some wore old, faded fatigues, while others were in newer regalia. Alex caught sight of a national park ranger, her distinctive hat visible above the crowd as she passed by, deep in discussion with a man in the sort of white overcoat a scientist might wear. There were groups of Regs, a medley of mechanics in coveralls, techies, medical staff, and plenty of civilians. They were gradually taking their seats on a motley collection of benches and fold-out chairs.

Alex spotted their parents and Abby together nearby and led his friends towards them. Iggy was there, too, talking with his mom Alice. The others greeted them but Iggy acted like they didn't exist.

"Any sign of Harriet?" Sol asked the group.

"Not yet," his father answered. "But they're working on it. I'm sure it's just a matter of time." His voice was reassuring, but Alex noticed that he didn't meet Sol's eyes.

"Alex!"

He spun around and smiled back at the young woman who'd spoken his name. She was about his age, with green eyes and light, copper-colored hair that curled into ringlets at the ends.

"Leah! You made it," he said as she leaned in for a hug.

"Of course I made it!" she replied.

"But I thought, when they attacked us in Hope—"

"That I'd been captured? Or worse? No way! Those chipslaves can't keep a good woman down." She smiled at Alex before turning to the others. "Sol, Tom, Abby, how are you guys?"

"Do I know you?" Tom asked, eyebrows raised.

"Yeah, you know her," Abby said, although she wasn't smiling. "It's Leah Mecon. She's from Hope. You know, the forest sanctuary? Her mom was mayor. Hi Leah," Abby said finally, looking from the young woman to Alex and back again.

Leah was about to reply when something behind them caught her eye.

"Iggy," she said quietly, looking at him intently as he stepped forward.

"Do I know you?" he asked, frowning as he rubbed his chin slowly.

"You don't remember me?" she asked, her face turning red. "Please say you remember me." Her voice sounded almost pleading.

"I'm not ... wait ... yeah, actually I think I do."

"Really?"

"Sure. I just had a flashback. There was a forest and a clearing in the trees and you were there and ... hey ... were we ... I mean, did we—"

"What? No ... yes ... I mean ... come over here and I'll explain." She took his hand and led him hastily to some seats a little way away, whispering to him urgently. A grin slowly spread across Iggy's handsome face as he stared at the attractive teenager beside him. Alex noticed that Iggy's mom, Alice, was frowning. Abby, however, looked pleased.

"So *that's* what happened!" she said, nodding. "I remember now." She was about to say something else to Alex when someone tapped her on the shoulder.

"Sybil! I can't believe it. Is it really you?" Abby asked, embracing her friend.

"In the flesh. How are Martha and Sally?"

"They were good when I last saw them," Abby replied. "Still controlled by their MeChips, though," she added, grimacing.

"Hey guys," Sybil said, turning to smile at the others.

"Do I know you?" Tom asked again uncertainly. "I definitely feel like I should know you."

"Yeah, you do," Sybil said, coloring slightly.

"And you said you know Sally and Martha?" Tom asked.

"Yeah. Abby, Martha, and Sally are my best friends."

"I'm dating Sally now," Tom said proudly.

"Oh ... but that's great!" Sybil said after a moment's pause. "It makes—"

"Hi everyone!"

Another young woman joined the group. She was tall with straight, coal-black hair and large, almond-shaped eyes.

"Electa, it's great to see you!" Alex said, recognizing her at once.

"Why don't I remember anyone?" Tom said plaintively. "Amnesia sucks."

"It'll all come back to you soon," Alex reassured him. "You already remembered Locke, right?"

"I guess. Hey, what's going on?" Tom asked, suddenly staring at Sybil and Electa uncertainly. Alex saw Tom's eyes dart downwards: the two girls were holding hands.

"Are you guys ... um ... together?"

"Yes," Sybil and Electa said firmly, both smiling as they caught one another's eye.

"And is that ... allowed?"

"Sure. Unless you're a chipslave," Electa said.

"The thing is," Sybil began, looking slightly embarrassed, "there's something else you should know, Tom—"

"And we've explained it to you already," Electa interrupted. "In Hope. You'll remember in time."

Tom opened his mouth to reply when his attention was drawn elsewhere. Following his friend's gaze, Alex turned and saw a group of people making their way from the back of the hangar down the center aisle towards a stage at the far end.

Alex didn't recognize the first few: several military types with fancy-looking uniforms and medals on their chests, followed by a couple more in white coats of the type worn by doctors or scientists. But the next few folks were familiar to him. First, his friend and mentor John Locke emerged, talking animatedly with General Slade Arnold. Alex scowled as he watched Arnold. He still didn't trust that man one bit. A moment later Leah's mom Jane Mecon and Captain Bailey from the town of Hope entered the room with another woman who was walking in the middle of their small group.

At first, Alex dismissed her as someone unimportant. She was the shortest member of the crowd that had just entered and unlike the generals she was dressed very simply, in blue jeans and a forest-green blouse. Her hair was gray and curly. She was chatting amiably with the others, her brown eyes sparkling as she looked from Jane Mecon to Captain Bailey and back again.

If she wasn't important, though, why did the other two seem to be hanging on her every word? And why did she look vaguely familiar? Had he met her before?

In a flash, Alex remembered. It was the woman behind the counter at Fran's Fooderia in Fairview, the town they'd visited to buy equipment for their failed effort to broadcast music to the nation. She'd been the proprietor of the café. But according to Locke, she was also something more than that. Before living in Fairview, Francesca Delano had also been the rightfully-elected President of the United States. Locke had explained to Alex how she had had her victory stolen from her by Bill Davison on the night of the election; the night the MeChips started controlling people.

No wonder the others were listening to her intently, Alex decided. He remembered how friendly she'd been when they'd spoken at the counter of her café, her brown eyes exuding affability and intelligence. The crowd fell silent as the group made its way to the front of the large room. Looking around, Alex saw everyone staring at this small, unassuming woman. Some had stood up or were craning their necks to see her, peering around or over those in front, so keen were they to catch sight of the president America had never had.

27 | Plan of Attack

The large crowd—more than a thousand people in all—watched in silence as the small group of leaders took their seats on the stage. One of the well-dressed soldiers started speaking into a microphone:

"My name is Brigadier General Smallwood and I am in charge of special military operations. We recently scored a vital success in our efforts to free our fine land from the MeChip and the evil dictator and so-called President, Davora Davison. A group of our operatives have liberated someone who will be critical to our work. She is the last surviving democratically-elected President of the United States, robbed of victory by President Davison Senior and the MeChip. She has agreed to lead our fight for freedom. I am proud to introduce President-elect Francesca Delano."

The small woman with gray curly hair stepped towards the microphone, smiling out at the crowd. Without a millisec's pause, the entire audience stood as one and began to applaud. Cheers rang out as they shouted their support for this diminutive figure who stood in front of them, eyes shining. There was something special about her, Alex thought as he stood on his tiptoes to catch a glimpse of her face. An unmistakable kindness and charisma radiated from her.

Unbidden, an image came to mind of Davora Davison when she had visited his school. She, too, had been cheered and adored by the crowd. But it had taken the MeChip's insidious influence to make people shout for her. Francesca Delano didn't need such subterfuge. Her leadership, her charm, was natural and real.

"Thank you for the warm welcome," she began at last. "I am so grateful to be here. I am also happy—very happy—to see so many of us have been freed from the MeChips' grasp. But our work has just begun. Most Americans remain enslaved."

"As many of you know, our attempts to break the MeChips' control through music have been frustrated. The enemy is now aware of that weakness and has taken steps to block it. Instead, our friends Dr. John Locke and General Slade Arnold have developed a new plan. Rather than short-circuiting the MeChips virtually through music, we plan to do two things at once. The first of these will be a series of diversionary measures to distract the enemy from our main plan. Brigadier General Smallwood, can you please tell us more?"

"Thank you, President Delano," the brigadier began. "We have found a way to break the MeChip control locally by disabling substations—the buildings that transmit and amplify the MeChips' power in a particular town or city neighborhood. We will attack six locations around the country simultaneously, take control of them, transmit the truth to the local population, and try to foment a series of small-scale rebellions."

"How many people can these substations reach?" came a voice from the crowd, hand raised.

"Up to 50,000 in each location," the brigadier answered.

"But that's not enough. There are 280 million people in America. What good will a few hundred thousand people do?"

"They will distract the enemy long enough to put our main plan into operation."

"Which is?" came the voice. The brigadier looked towards General Slade Arnold, who stood up and took the microphone. Muttering broke out among some in the crowd and Alex wondered if they, like him, mistrusted this man. Was he really on their side, or was his apparent conversion part of some cunning plan to defeat the revolution from within?

"Our plan is to take over the MeChip's main control center, to free people of its influence, and then to communicate the truth to the entire population," General Arnold said as soon as the muttering subsided.

"And where is the control center?" came another voice from the crowd.

"At the heart of the spider's web," Arnold replied, pausing for a moment before adding: "In Washington, D.C. ... underneath the White House."

28 | Defeat

Alex peeked around the corner, saw the two Fixers and drew back. His team had already come far, penetrating deep into enemy territory. Using the power of a new MeChip, which had recently been inserted in the back of his neck, he sent out invisible tendrils of light around the corner towards his foes. His mind connected with their MeChips, pulling up their details in the corner of his retina. He probed again, aware that Abby, Iggy, Locke, and several soldiers were close behind him, each gripping a laz-pistol and remote-control device.

"What's taking so long?" Iggy hissed. "Can't you hurry it up any?"

Alex held up a hand for silence as the thin coils of light emanating from his MeChip found their way into the Fixers' minds.

Place your weapons on the ground. Place your weapons on the ground, he instructed them, his thoughts feeding forcefully into their subconscious.

Alex snuck another glance around the corner, saw one of the Fixers take his weapon out of his holster and place it on the concrete floor. The other, however, seemed to be fighting Alex's control. He had drawn his weapon but was holding it uncertainly, mumbling to himself and evidently unsure what to do.

"This is taking too long," Iggy said, "I'm gonna take care of it." He brushed past Alex and stepped around the corner.

"No, wait," Alex said taking a step forward and trying to pull Iggy back, his concentration broken.

Fzzoom! Fzzoom! Iggy's laz-pistol erupted, two beams of light smashing into one of the Fixers, who slumped to the ground. But the other Fixer, the one who'd been fighting Alex's control, began blasting back. One beam caught Iggy in the shoulder, sending him staggering. The man ran down the corridor and punched a red button on the wall. A moment later a siren began to wail, its earsplitting sound insistent as it screeched its warning over and over.

Locke hurried forward and pressed buttons on his remote, freezing the Fixer in place. Abby had dashed towards Iggy. He was leaning against the wall, breathing heavily.

Alex heard the tramp of heavy boots. He whirled around as at least a dozen soldiers rushed into the corridor, weapons raised.

"Retreat," he urged the others. Turning to run, he stopped as more troops advanced from the way they'd just come. They were trapped.

"Drop your weapons!" the leading trooper shouted as a score more laz-rifles pointed at them. Defeated, Alex and the others placed their weapons on the ground and raised their hands over their heads.

"My fault? No way! It was you—you're just too slow," Iggy said accusingly.

"What was the rush?" Alex countered, glaring at him from across the table. "Better to take our time than go too quickly and mess up. Right John?" Alex asked, turning to Locke.

"Alex is right, Iggy. *Festina lente.*"

"Fez Tina-what-now?"

"*Festina lente.* It's Latin. It means 'more haste, less speed.'"

"Nope, you've still lost me," Iggy said dismissively, shrugging like he didn't care.

"It means you will advance more quickly towards your goal if you take your time and do the job right," Locke said.

"We're lucky this was just a training session," Abby added, looking at Iggy and shaking her head. "Imagine if this was the real thing?"

"Well it wasn't, was it?" Iggy replied obstinately, folding his arms across his chest. "And I still say we could have picked up the pace and—"

"Iggy, if you insist on acting in such a reckless manner, I will have no choice but to take you off our team," Locke said firmly. "We have the most important mission of all in front of us—breaking into the White House and taking over the underground complex where the MeChip central command is located. It will take guile and cunning, not the bulldozer approach you seem to favor."

"But you need me," Iggy said, looking smug. "Being able to control people's MeChips will be important on this mission. You said it yourself. And I'm the best at it." Iggy leaned back in his chair, hands behind his head, grinning at the group.

"You're not the best at it!" Alex shot back.

"I am. You don't count."

"Why not?"

"Because you've been practicing this for ages. We're all new. And among the newbies, I'm the best."

"That's not the point," Alex replied. "Besides, Abby did better than you."

"Did not!"

"Gentlemen, enough," Locke interrupted, sounding exasperated. "All three of you have shown extraordinary abilities with your MeChips, which is why you were all selected for this mission. But I will remove you from the team if you do not follow my orders. Do you understand?" Locke said, scowling at Iggy.

"Fine, fine!" Iggy replied, hands raised. "So, any word from my fa—I mean, from General Arnold?"

"You may call him your father, Iggy. We all remember who he is," Locke said, his voice gentler now.

"Fine. Any news from him?"

"Not for the past 24 hours," Locke replied, frowning slightly. "But when we last heard he was back in the White House making arrangements with a few trusted people to help us gain access. Now, let us take a break and pick things up in an hour, shall we? We only have three days left and we need to keep training."

The four of them rose to leave. Iggy strode off instantly but Alex hung back. He was hoping to talk with Abby, but before he could speak she had turned to Locke.

"John, can we talk? Somewhere private?"

"Of course. This way, Abby," the old man replied. The two of them departed quickly, Abby whispering rapidly to Locke as they left. Alex was suddenly alone.

Giving them a minute's head start, Alex slowly made his way down the corridor, trudging towards the mess hall. He was feeling frustrated and disappointed.

First, their preparations had not been going well. For the first few days after they'd arrived at the base, they had been given basic weapons training as well as tests to see how well they could control their MeChips. Dr. Locke had speculated that others might be able to use their MeChips to control their enemies just as Alex had, which would be a very useful skill in the battles to come. As a result, almost every single person at the base had undergone trials, using MeChips connected to a local network that could not be hacked by their enemies.

While most people could gain some level of control over their own MeChips in time, it turned out that the ability to project influence onto others was rare. In fact, only the teenagers at the camp had demonstrated this skill. Locke had said it had something to do with the greater adaptability of young people's minds. Neuroplasticity, he'd called it. But whether it was this or something else, the young people could do it while the older ones could not. Of those, Abby and Iggy had picked up the skill quickest, quickly joining Alex as the strongest in the group. Tom, Sol, Leah, Sybil, Electa, and the handful of other teenagers on the base all showed potential. But Abby and Iggy were clearly ahead of the rest.

They'd therefore been chosen—along with John Locke and half-a-dozen elite special forces soldiers—to join the biggest mission of all: infiltrating the MeChip control center under the White House. Their training had been going on for a week. But Alex couldn't pretend it was going well. First, working with Iggy was frustrating. While he was undoubtedly talented and athletic, he was a hothead and tended to rush things. Secondly, none of them seemed to be able to fully control others with their MeChips. Even Alex, who'd had the most practice using it, was sometimes unable to exert complete control over the Fixers and other troops they'd met in the mock-up of the White House basements. Sometimes, the Fixers fought back.

Alex entered the mess hall. It was a little early for lunch and the place was almost empty except for Leah and Iggy, who were sitting in the corner, their heads close together as they whispered what Alex presumed were sweet nothings to each other. They didn't even notice him. Alex shook his head, wondering for the hundredth time what a smart girl like Leah saw in a guy like Iggy.

Grabbing a soda, he sat down at the far end of the room. His mind drifted back to Abby. He was feeling frustrated and discouraged about her, too. Alex was very keen to talk to her alone, to find out how much she remembered about their conversations in the tree house and the forest.

Did she still have feelings for him? At this point, Alex had absolutely no clue. The training had been so intense since they'd arrived at the base that it seemed like they never had time to talk. Whatever spare time Abby had was spent with her mom, Susanna.

Alex didn't blame her for that. After all, Abby had just lost her father ... or at least, the man she'd thought of as her father. Susanna and Abby must be in mourning. Had either of them remembered that the man who'd been shot wasn't really who he was supposed to be? Did Abby know her real dad had died some months ago? If so, had that made their grief worse? More complicated, perhaps? And why had Abby asked to talk with Locke just now? Come to think of it, Locke seemed to be with Susanna and Abby a lot these days. What was all that about?

Speaking of Locke, Alex was keen to speak with him, too. He had so many questions to ask, so much he wanted to know. Why were Susanna and Abby monopolizing all of the old man's time?

Alex's thoughts drifted to his friends Sol and Tom. Sol was already gone, out on some secret mission he hadn't been allowed to talk about. Meanwhile, Tom was training with the team that would make a diversionary attack on the West Coast's regional headquarters in San Francisco. Tom had been working day and night on preparations and although they were sharing the same room, the two of them had both been so busy they'd hardly had time to exchange a word. Still, Alex knew he should feel grateful. At least they'd been allowed to join these military operations. Locke had told him they needed everyone on board, even the teenagers. The rebels might fill a small airbase, but there were still precious few of them for what they were trying to do: defeat an enemy who controlled millions of people.

Finishing his drink, Alex stood up. He was about to leave when a woman entered the room. She was tall with curly gray hair and dark skin, high cheekbones, and fine features. She was wearing an ancient leather jacket. Her lips were moving, as if she was talking to herself under her breath. She looked around the almost-empty room, her eyes open wide as they darted from the kitchen where the meals were prepared to the metal plates that would hold the food, buffet style, to the many tables and chairs around the almost-empty mess hall. Her eyes alighted on Alex and she approached him slowly, frowning a little.

"I ... I know you. Don't I?" she asked uncertainly.

"Yes," Alex replied, eyes wide in surprise. "And I know you."

29 | Locke's Girlfriend

"It's Maggie Corbin, isn't it?" Alex began. "We met in the forest, Maggie. You were living in a tower."

"Yes. That's where I used to live." Her voice was quiet and she spoke slowly. Her eyes flickered away from his and darted around the room, finally settling on the piano.

"But ... what are you doing here?" Alex asked, confused at her sudden appearance at the base.

"John sent friends to get me."

"John Locke?"

"Yes. A couple days ago. They came to get me. There were three of them. Dressed in green. I was scared at first. I tried to hide, but they found me. They told me I'd be safe. We walked for a long time and then they put me in a vehicle and we drove for a while and now ... here I am," she said, her eyes wandering again around the cafeteria.

"Why did he send people to find you?" Alex asked curiously.

"I don't know. But he did."

"Well ... I'm glad you're safe," Alex said at last.

"Am I safe? I feel ... I don't know ... lost. I miss my home ... my tower. But it's gone now. Where are we, anyway?"

"We're at a military base. And yes, you're safe."

"I don't trust the military. They chased me once."

"You can trust the people here. I promise," Alex said, trying to sound reassuring. "How's your dog?" Alex asked, remembering Maggie's oversized canine companion and how Sybil had petted him.

"They shot him," Maggie said sadly, still looking at the piano, her voice dropping even lower.

"Locke's friends shot your dog?" Alex asked in shock. "Why would they do that?"

"No! Not John. Never John. It was before that. A few months ago, maybe? Or a few weeks? I don't know. Some other people did it. Soldiers too, I guess. They were searching for John, I think. And for you, maybe. They blew up my tower. And they chased us. I got away, but they ... they got Pete ..." Her voice trailed off and she continued staring at the piano, evidently lost in thought. A solitary tear welled up in one eye and trailed down her face. She didn't wipe it away.

"I'm sorry. He was a nice dog," Alex said at last.

"He was, wasn't he?" she replied, the ghost of a smile flickering across her face as she looked back at Alex at last, her eyes suddenly more alive. "He was old, though. I don't think he'd have made it through another winter even if they hadn't ... they hadn't ..."

Her voice drifted off again and her eyes slid away from his and back to the piano.

"John told us that he knew you," Alex said, remembering something John Locke had said. "Is that right?"

"Of course I know John," she replied, her voice now dreamlike and distant.

She was silent for so long, her eyes still fixed on the piano, that Alex thought the conversation was ended. Then she looked directly at him once more, her voice suddenly firm and clear:

"Clarissa should never have broken up with him. I told her that."

"I'm sorry ... what?"

"Clarissa. My older sister," Maggie declared, looking at Alex as if he'd missed something obvious.

"Your sister ... dated Dr. Locke?"

"She dated John, yes. I told her not to break up with him. But she didn't listen. She never listened to me. That's why we stopped talking in the end."

"And ... um ... when was this?" Alex asked, feeling like he was definitely missing something.

"Oh, ages ago. Years and years back. Decades, probably. But I told Clarissa, sure it's hard having a long-distance thing, but he loves you and he won't be at college forever, then he'll be back and you can pick right up again where you left off. But she didn't want to wait and then she moved to LA and met that other guy Mike—who wasn't good enough for her in my opinion, which I told her straight out—and then she came back years later with a child, which she told everyone was Mike's, but by then we'd fallen out and I was living in New York and I didn't get back to Lincoln for a long time, and by the time I did Clarissa was ... she was ..."

Maggie Corbin delivered her story rapid fire, the words cascading out like a dam bursting its banks. Finally, though, she trailed off into silence once more. She looked away from Alex, her eyes drifting back to the piano again.

"She was what?" Alex asked curiously.

"Dead. She was dead."

"Oh. I'm sorry."

"Him too."

"What? Who?"

"Her boyfriend Mike. He died, too. They were both in the car when it happened. It was a head on collision. Clarissa always said Mike drove too fast."

"They both died in a car crash?" Alex asked, trying to keep up with the story.

"That's what I said. Their daughter was the only survivor."

They were both silent as Alex processed this information.

"So they ... they left a baby daughter?" he asked at last.

"Yeah. Only she wasn't a baby by then. She was probably—I don't know—twelve, maybe?"

"And what happened to her?"

"She had to go into a foster home, I think. At least, that's what I heard, since I was still in New York. If I could go back in time, I would've come back to Lincoln and helped out. But I was too busy with my own life—too selfish, I guess."

"But you lived in Lincoln later?" Alex asked, remembering what Locke had told them about Maggie when they were in the forest.

"Yes. I moved back to Lincoln in the end. Clarissa's daughter was all grown up by then, though. I should've got in touch, but I didn't. I was going through a hard time then and ... I don't know. But I heard nice things about her. She got married and everything. She even had a daughter of her own. Which makes me a great aunt, I guess."

"Oh ... that's nice," Alex replied, not sure what to say.

"I guess. I really should have made contact. But then everything was going wrong for me, somehow, and I ended up living in the forest. Just Pete and me. So I never got to meet my niece ... or my niece's daughter."

"Maybe you can still meet her one day," Alex said, trying to look on the bright side.

"I wish I could," Maggie said, smiling for the first time. "I'd love to meet my niece. I bet Susanna's just great!"

30 | Reunited

"Wait ... what? Maggie, did you say your niece's name is Susanna?" Alex asked, his mind suddenly racing.

"That's what I heard."

"And Susanna had a daughter, too?"

"Yes. A few years ago now, I guess."

"Do you know how long ago, exactly?"

"No. I lost track of time these past few years."

"Is she a teenager yet? Susanna's daughter, I mean."

"She might be," Maggie shrugged.

"Do you remember her name?"

"No. My memory ain't as good as it was. All those years of just Pete and me in the forest, I guess. And I wasn't well before that, either, to tell the truth."

"Can you try to remember? It's important," Alex said as a suspicion grew in his mind about who it might be.

"Was it Bailey, maybe? No, that's not right. Or Audrey? No, that doesn't sound right, either," Maggie said, frowning.

"It's not *Abby*, is it?" Alex asked.

"Yeah, that's what it was. Abby!" Her face brightened. "Susanna's daughter is called Abby. You know her?"

"I know Abby *and* Susanna. They're my neighbors back in Lincoln!" Alex declared, shocked at the coincidence.

Maggie didn't speak for several seconds. She just stood staring at Alex, shaking her head in disbelief.

"If you see them, will you tell them about me?" Maggie asked at last. "Tell them they have family asking after them?"

"I can do better than that," Alex replied, smiling. "They're here at the base, too. Sit down here, Maggie. I'll bring them to you right now."

Alex dashed out of the mess hall and down the corridor, determined to find them. He didn't have far to go. In fact, he almost collided with Susanna and Abby as he tore around a corner. They were walking with John Locke. The three of them were smiling, although Abby frowned as Alex darted towards them.

"Hey, watch we're you're ... oh, Alex!" she declared as he pulled up just in front of them. "Why the rush?"

"Just the people I was looking for!" Alex replied with a grin. "There's someone who wants to meet you. She's in the cafeteria."

"We were just on our way there," Susanna replied. "Who is it?"

"You should find out for yourself," Alex smiled. "Come on."

Frowning, Susanna, Abby and Locke joined Alex as he retraced his steps back down the corridor and into the mess hall.

"Maggie, you've arrived," John Locke said as soon as he saw her.

Maggie Corbin stood up as John Locke strode forward and gave her a hug. "When did you get here?"

"Earlier today," Maggie replied. Then her eyes fixed on Susanna.

"Susanna. Is that you?" she asked uncertainly.

"Do I know you?" Susanna replied, pulling up short.

"We met in the forest," Maggie said, ignoring the question. "You were there with John, weren't you? I should have known it was you, Susanna. And you, Abby. You know ... you look like your grandma. *Just* like her."

"I never knew my grandma," Abby replied, frowning.

"But *I* did," Maggie replied emphatically, beaming at them at last. "Go on, John. Tell them. Tell them who I am."

"I think you should have the pleasure of doing that," Locke said, smiling back at her.

"Okay, then I will. Susanna ... I'm your mother's sister. I'm your aunt Maggie."

"You're my ... aunt?"

"That's right," Maggie replied, still smiling and shaking her head, as if she couldn't believe what was happening. "I'm your aunt."

For a few millisecs no one moved. Then Maggie stepped forward and wrapped her arms around Susanna who, after a moment's hesitation, hugged her back. Finally, Maggie turned to Abby and embraced her, too.

"But this is unbelievable!" Susanna said at last. "First, I meet my real father. Now I meet my aunt."

"What? Mike's here? But Mike's dead, dear," Maggie said, looking around and frowning.

"I know that. I mean John," Susanna replied, turning to Locke as her smile broadened.

"But John ain't your dad, Susanna," Maggie stated flatly as she shook her head. "Mike is."

"No, Maggie," John Locke said. "We all thought Mike was Susanna's father. But it turns out that ... well ... that *I* am."

"Wait ... *you're* Susanna's father?" Alex asked, unable to believe what he was hearing.

Locke nodded.

"You can't be," Maggie insisted. "She was with Mike in LA when Susanna was born. I remember. Mike *must* be the father."

"That's what I thought, too," Locke replied. "I never even suspected Susanna might be my child. When Clarissa broke up with me and moved to LA, she cut me off completely. But it turns out she was already pregnant when she left Lincoln ... with *my* child."

"What? Why didn't she tell you?" Maggie asked, looking confused.

"I have no idea. You know how headstrong she could be," John said, shaking his head slowly. "She must have decided to bring the child up by herself. I don't suppose I'll ever know why. Of course, I heard on the grapevine that she'd met this man, Mike, in LA. And when I found out later that she'd had a daughter, I assumed he was the father. Why wouldn't he be? It was only when I was living back in Lincoln decades years later and fortuitously learned Susanna's age that I began to suspect. A secret DNA test a few years ago finally told me the truth."

"Is that when you told Susanna who you really were?" Alex asked curiously.

"No," Locke admitted. "I couldn't when she was still under the MeChip's control. What good would it have done? I only told Susanna and Abby who I was very recently."

"I wish my mom had told us the truth all those years ago, John," Susanna said, looking at Locke sadly.

"She always was pigheaded, that sister of mine," Maggie said. "Always thought she knew best."

"She must have had her reasons for not telling anyone," Locke said slowly.

"But we're together now," Susanna said, beaming.

Alex could barely believe what he was hearing. Suddenly, he had another realization. He turned to Abby:

"Wait ... but if John is Susanna's father, that also makes him—"

"My grandfather!" Abby declared. "Wild, isn't it?" Abby added, smiling at Alex for the first time in days.

"No way!" came a voice. Alex spun around and saw Iggy staring at them in disbelief, Leah by his side. "Abby, I feel sorry for you. Imagine having this old fossil as a relative!"

"At least she doesn't have a murderer as a father!" Alex shot back.

"Say that again, dexter!" Iggy dared him, squaring up to his adversary.

"Iggy, no! We're leaving. Right now," Leah said, tugging on his arm. "Dr. Locke, Susanna, Abby, I'm so sorry. He doesn't mean it," Leah said, her face bright red. Alex was surprised to see that Iggy didn't resist as she took his hand and led him from the room, chastising him in an undertone as they walked away.

"That boy was very rude!" Maggie Corbin said, watching Iggy's retreating back as he left the mess hall.

"He does need to learn better manners," Locke admitted, "although in his defense, he's been through a lot lately. He, too, recently learned more about his family, which came as a shock to him."

"I just can't believe you're all related," Alex said, turning to look at Abby, Susanna, John Locke and Maggie Corbin and shaking his head in disbelief.

"Amazing, isn't it? Three generations of us, right here," Abby said, still smiling at him.

Just then, a nurse entered the cafeteria. He spotted Maggie and rushed forward.

"There you are, Ms. Corbin. We wondered where you'd gotten to. We were so worried about you. We have to bring you back to the medical wing. We haven't even given you a proper medical yet."

"But I don't want to go. I just found my family!" Maggie Corbin protested.

"That may be, but we need to finish your medical and keep you under observation for a while. You've been through a lot lately and—"

"It's alright," Locke said, speaking up. "She really has found her family at long last. We'll bring her back to you in half an hour, if that's alright?"

"Thirty minutes, then," the nurse agreed after a moment's hesitation, "then straight back. Okay?"

"Of course," Locke reassured him.

As the nurse departed, John Locke, Susanna, Abby and Maggie made their way to the nearest table, chatting animatedly among themselves.

"You guys must have a lot to catch up on so I'll ... um ... leave you to it," Alex said, still only half able to process what he'd just seen and heard.

No one replied. They were already deep in conversation.

After a millisec's hesitation, Alex turned to leave.

31 | Ready

Place your weapons on the ground.

Alex's instruction to the Fixers' MeChips was calm and clear. Ignoring Iggy and the others behind him, he focused completely on the two enemies ahead.

Place your weapons on the ground. Place your weapons on the ground. This time, the two Fixers complied.

People are about to enter the corridor. They are friends. Do not worry. They are friends.

Once more, the message from his MeChip to theirs was relaxed and reassuring. But had it worked? Alex risked a quick peak around the corner. At least one of the Fixers was smiling; a good sign. Motioning to the others, he started up the corridor, his remote control at the ready.

"Don't worry, we're friends," he said out loud, smiling. The two men grinned back.

A moment later, Locke and Abby had incapacitated them with their remotes. While the six special forces soldiers on their team scouted ahead, Iggy and Alex put cuffs on their foes' hands and feet, gagged them, and sat them down. The two Fixers did not resist, their minds disabled by Locke's gadget, their chins lolling onto their chests.

The group approached the next corridor.

"Where now?" Iggy asked.

"Left," Locke replied. The group made its way cautiously along the corridor but met no one else. Finally, they reached a small metal door set in the side of the concrete wall.

"And this is where General Arnold will meet us and let us into the tunnel that leads under the White House," Locke said, turning to the group.

"So we did it?" Alex asked.

"Yes, Locke replied with a smile. "Arnold should have cleared the way for us and will guide us to the MeChip headquarters. Nice job, everyone."

"So the training's done?" Iggy asked.

"Yes, but I'd like to have one more successful run-through before we leave tomorrow."

"Fine," Iggy sighed. "When?"

"Let's say 1500."

"In English?" Iggy asked, raising an eyebrow.

"3 p.m."

"Fine. I'm off to see Leah." He walked away without a backwards glance. A moment later, the special forces troops followed in the same direction, leaving Alex, Abby, and Locke alone. Once more, Alex looked at the two of them. He was still having trouble processing that John Locke was Abby's grandfather. Did Locke's family connections explain why he had been so focused on their town and even their high school? It definitely explained why the old man had formed a bond with Abby and Susanna in the forest, even if it didn't account for why Locke had contacted *him*. Was there more to the story? Alex felt like one or two pieces of the jigsaw were still missing.

The three of them made their way to the mess hall. The place was almost empty, although the same nurse as before was sitting at the piano, playing another tune from the Retro-Before Time. Abby and Alex grabbed sodas from the fridge while Locke served himself a cup of coffee.

"Have you heard from Arnold lately?" Alex asked as they sat down.

"Last night," Locke replied, sipping at his drink.

"And the President doesn't suspect he's changed sides?"

"Apparently not. But I'm—"

"The piano's free. I'm going to play," Abby stood up and made her way to the instrument as the nurse left the room. A millisec later and her fingers were caressing the keys as she played a classic Rock Shop number. The original version was loud and insistent, but Abby's rendition was gentler, more soothing. Locke and Alex sat in silence for some time listening to her. Alex's fingers twitched. He was itching to get hold of a guitar again.

"She really is very good, don't you agree?" Locke asked, eyes twinkling.

"Stellar," Alex concurred. They sat for a while longer before Alex spoke again.

"I still can't believe you're her grandfather."

"Yes, it was something of a shock when I uncovered the truth," Locke admitted.

"You must be happy to be reunited with her and her mom."

"Indescribably. Once our glorious revolution is over, I hope to spend as much time with them as I can."

"Can I ask you a question?" Alex asked hesitantly, while Abby continued to play. Locke nodded, his eyes still fixed on his granddaughter.

"Why did you contact me and not Abby? In the beginning, I mean."

"I already told you, Alex. You are a very gifted musician and I felt you could help me with my aim of breaking the MeChip's control."

"Abby's a stellar musician, too."

"That is true," Locke said. "Perhaps I chose you because I was afraid to involve Abby in my plans. She is my granddaughter, after all. Maybe I wanted to keep her safe," Locke replied, still looking at Abby.

"What about Iggy, then? He's a great musician, too. He's the one who won the Best Band contest after all, not me. I froze in my first competition. Why not pick him—a proven winner?"

"Aside from the fact that I believe in *you*, Alex, I would have thought my reason for not considering Iggy would now be obvious."

"You mean, because of who his father is?"

"Exactly. Since I knew Arnold was occasionally checking up on me, I did not wish to arouse his suspicions by showing any interest at all in his son or his musical gifts."

"So you knew Iggy was General Arnold's son?"

"Yes."

"But ... how? There's more to this whole story, isn't there?" Alex asked. "Something you're still not telling me."

"Yes," Locke said after a pause. "But it's really not my place to say more. This secret belongs to someone else."

"But *you're* involved in it, aren't you?"

"Yes," Locke said, still watching his granddaughter as she sat at the piano.

"And I'm involved, too ... aren't I?" Alex added, as an odd hunch—an intuition he couldn't quite explain—intruded into his thoughts.

"In a way," Locke admitted, still avoiding Alex's gaze.

"Then can you please tell me? After everything we've been through, don't you owe me that?"

"Very well," Locke said at last. "You do deserve the truth, Alex, so I'll do my best. Where to begin? Let me see ... did your mother ever talk about her childhood?"

"Not much," Alex said, trying to remember. "She grew up in Lincoln, right?"

"Yes. But she wasn't born there. In fact, she was born a very long way away."

"Really?"

"Yes. Her family moved to Lincoln from England when she was four and—"

"Alex! Alex!"

He looked up as someone burst into the mess hall and rushed towards him.

It was Sol. He had a cut across his forehead. His clothes were torn and dirty.

And he had the biggest grin Alex had ever seen plastered across his face.

32 | Sol's Mission

"We did it! We got her," his friend declared, hugging Alex so hard he squeezed the breath out of him.

"Did what? Got who?" Alex asked as Sol drew away, still beaming.

"Harriet, of course! Who else? That's where I've been. Helping extract her."

"Extract her? From where?"

"From Lincoln jail. And we got Sally and Martha, too. Come on, they're in the medical wing." Without waiting, Sol rushed off down the corridor. Alex hurried after him, Locke and Abby close behind.

A couple of minutes later they were in a room crowded with patients, doctors, and nurses. Alex followed Sol through the crowd. Harriet was in the far corner, lying on a hospital bed. A nurse was fussing over her.

"I'm fine, I'm fine," she insisted. "Go help my parents. They're the ones who need taking care of."

"Harriet, look who's here," Sol said as he rushed forward, taking her hand in his.

Abby hugged her friend gently, being careful not to detach the wires hooking her up to various machines, as well as the intravenous bag dripping a clear fluid through a tube into her arm.

"Hi Abby, Hi Alex," Harriet said, mustering a smile. "How are you?"

"Better for seeing you. Are you okay?" Abby asked, looking with concern at her friend, who appeared thin and fatigued.

"I'll survive," she said, coughing a little.

"Abby!" Sally and Martha stepped out from behind a bedside screen. They looked better than their friend and it was obvious they'd already been discharged by the medical staff.

"What happened?" Alex asked as they all embraced.

"It's all a bit fuzzy," Harriet began. "The Regs arrived at our house a couple of weeks ago and told us we had to go to jail. Then some people arrived—I guess they were friends of yours—and tried to help us escape, but the Regs shot them. Once they'd locked us up, they started asking us all sorts of questions, mostly about you, John," she said, looking over the others at Locke. "It was all pretty bad ..."

"They only arrested Martha and me a couple of days ago," Sally added, taking up the story and nodding towards her friend. "They didn't explain why at first. Then they started asking us lots of weird questions. It was frightening."

"But Sol arrived early this morning with some soldiers. There was a fight and he managed to free us," Martha added.

"He was really brave," Harriet chimed in, looking lovingly at her boyfriend and squeezing his hand.

"They all were. One of your soldiers was ... was shot. But in the end, we got away. Then Sol took out our MeChips and explained what was going on," Martha said, looking as if she might cry.

"You're safe now," Abby said, putting an arm around her friend. "We all are."

"Is Tom here?" Sally asked, looking around the room as a tinge of pink appeared in her cheeks.

"I couldn't find him," Sol said. "I think he's training. But I'm sure he'll be—"

"I'm here!" Tom said, pushing through the crowd. He stopped as he saw Sally. The two stared at each for a moment, as if frozen to the spot. Then, at the exact same time, they threw themselves into each other's arms, lips locking together, oblivious to the stares and smiles of those around them.

"I guess they're happy to see each other," Harriet said, grinning at last.

"Not as happy as I was to see you," Sol said, leaning in to kiss her gently on the lips.

"I'm just going to ... um ... ask the doctor a question," Martha said, reddening slightly and avoiding Alex and Abby's gaze.

"Yeah, I should go, too," Alex said. "Um ... I'll catch you later, guys," he added. Neither of the couples replied.

Alex turned and looked for Locke, but he was deep in conversation with one of the nurses.

"I'm going back to the cafeteria. I want to play that stellar piano again before lunch. Wanna come?" Abby looked at Alex, who nodded. Together, they made their way through the crowd.

"I'm so glad they're safe," Abby said as they walked along the corridor.

"Me too. I hope Harriet's okay, though. She looked a little beat up."

"She'll be fine. She's a fighter."

"We won't have long to hang out with them. Can you believe we leave on our mission tomorrow?"

"Not really. The time has gone by so fast. Are you nervous?"

"Terrified. You?"

"Same. But I'm determined not to let my fears stop me. This is too important."

"There's one bit that's giving me the jeepsters more than anything," Alex admitted.

"What's that?"

"Slade Arnold. So much depends on him, but I still don't trust him."

"I feel the same way. But John believes in him. I guess that has to be enough."

Alex was smiling to himself as he headed down the corridor a couple of hours later. He'd gotten to hang out with Abby and listen to her play before everyone came into the mess hall for lunch. Then he'd caught up with Tom and Sol, who were both thrilled at being reunited with their girlfriends. Now, Alex just needed to change back into his army fatigues before 3 p.m. If they could do one more successful practice of the mission, he'd almost feel ready for what lay ahead of them in Washington, D.C.

Almost.

Alex had just turned into the corridor where their sleeping quarters were located when the sound of voices up ahead made him stop.

"Look, Mom, I'm glad I have a dad and all, but can we really trust him?"

"I'm not sure, Iggy. I think so, but only time will tell. I want to believe him when he says he's changed."

"Me too. But it's hard. I mean, he lied, Mom. He lied to you. And he left us—you and me—alone for so long."

"You're right, Iggy. I can't deny it."

"Then how can you forgive him for that?"

"I haven't. Not yet. Slade Arnold has a lot to prove. But he promised me that he's changed. He promised it would be different this time."

"And what if he's fooling us? What if he's fooling everyone here?"

"Then we'll lose, Iggy. But so will he."

"What will he lose, Mom? If he's fooling all of us and he's still on the President's side, they'll beat us for sure. And what will he lose then?"

"Us, Iggy. He'll lose us. And this time he'll lose us forever."

Slowly, Alex backed off down the corridor the way he'd come. The voices continued, but this was not a conversation Alex felt he should be hearing. It was private, after all. Besides, he'd heard enough already. If Iggy and Alice didn't fully trust Slade Arnold, why should he?

In spite of the warmth in the building, Alex shivered. What if they were walking into a trap? What if their mission to D.C. and their fight against the MeChip ended in disaster?

33 | Memories and Music

"Alex, can we talk?"

Alex looked up from his book. He'd been alone in his room, trying to relax after their final training session. It had gone well and he knew he should feel good about it. Still, his fears about General Arnold kept intruding. How could anyone trust him? Sighing, he put the book to one side and motioned for them to come in.

"What's up, guys?" He looked from his mom to the man everyone thought was his dad. His mom had that lopsided smile she wore when she was nervous about something. His so-called father looked serious, brows knitted.

"Alex, we need to tell you something," his mom began. "The thing is, your father ... that is ... Ben and I recently remembered something about who we are. You see, Ben is not—"

"Not my dad? I already know."

"We figured you might. It's been hard for us these last few days. Very hard. But we've decided to—"

"—give your relationship a chance? I figured that out, too," Alex said.

"You seem to know everything," his mom replied, her smile suddenly more genuine. "And yes, we think there's something for us to build on, something special here. After all, we've been together five years already, even if we didn't know who Ben really was. But we're worried about you, Alex. How does all of this make you feel?"

"I feel really sad about my dad," Alex said at last. "I can't believe he's been gone so long. But I've had more time than you to get my head around things. More time to grieve. I think I'll be okay now. I have to be, right?"

"And how do you feel about your mother and I being together?" asked the man everyone called Ben.

"I think it's the right decision."

"You do?" asked Ben, eyebrows raised.

"Sure. Look, you've already been together five years. You were both deceived by the MeChip, both fed lies about who you are. But you've been happy together and I have a feeling you'd have been happy even without the MeChip influencing you. You've been a good parent to me, too. I have no complaints about how you treated me or my mom, Ben. I'm glad you have each other."

His mom rushed forward and hugged him, sobbing. Alex felt a tear in his eye, too, but wiped it away before it could show. As his mom drew back, Alex turned to face Ben. The man held out his hand to shake Alex's.

For a moment Alex paused. Then, ignoring the hand, he leaned in and hugged him, too. Finally, Ben drew back, smiling at last. He was about to speak when Tom rushed in.

"Alex, Alex ... oh, hi guys," he said, acknowledging Liz and Ben before turning back to his friend. "Guess what?"

"You finally disentangled yourself from Sally?" Alex said with a smirk.

"Oh, that ... yeah. Isn't she stellar? And so tidy!" he declared with a grin.

"Is that what you came to tell me?"

"Yeah. But there's more. Sol found some instruments in an old storage room. We thought we could play again. Are you in?"

"Smeck yeah!" Alex said, beaming back at his friend.

"See you later, Alex," his mom said as he made to leave. "And thank you."

"Are we ready? Then let's do this. One, two, ah-one, two, three, four," Tom intoned as his sticks hit the drums, laying down a light beat. Sol started slapping his bass guitar and added a deep layer to the rhythm section for a full sixteen bars, quietly at first before rising up in a crescendo of sound. Next, Abby chimed in on the keyboard, throwing down a series of sampled horn "stabs" on the one-beat as the decibels continued to rise.

Finally, Alex strummed his guitar and started to sing:
"Get up and dance,
Get on down while you have the chance,
Come on and sing,
Just forget about everything ..."

Alex scanned the crowd. There were hundreds in the hangar, drawn by the news of an impromptu performance. Old and young were moving in time with the music as Alex's vocals rang out loud and clear. Everyone knew this Rock Shop song. It was catchy and upbeat, one of those joyful tunes that helped you forget your worries for a while. And with so many of these people leaving on dangerous missions soon, no wonder the audience was keen to leave its troubles behind for a night.

Alex spotted President Francesca Delano dancing with Locke, Captain Bailey, and Brigadier General Smallwood, while a group of twentysomethings were laughing and singing nearby. The only person who didn't seem to be enjoying himself was Iggy. He was sitting in the corner, a scowl on his face. Alex didn't blame him. The situation with his newly-discovered father Slade Arnold would have been enough to confuse anyone. Not only that, but Iggy's girlfriend Leah had already left on her mission, along with Sybil, Electa, and dozens of others. He must be worried about her, Alex realized.

But Alex was having too much fun to feel sorry for his old adversary. It felt so good—so right—to hold a guitar in his hands once again. There and then, Alex made a promise to himself: if they came through this last mission in one piece, he would never let a single day pass by without playing music.

34 | The Journey

Alex looked out the window at the passing scenery. Over the five-day journey, the bus had crossed between mountains, seemingly-endless fields of soybeans and corn, and, finally, forested hills and valleys. They had stayed each night in a different motel, their group of 40 people filing into out-of-the-way accommodation that seemed deserted except for a handful of service staff. On each occasion, it was obvious they had been expected and that those who welcomed them were converts to their cause. Clearly, the revolution was bigger than he had realized.

Alex had been hoping to talk with Locke again, but he was always up the front of the coach with Francesca Delano, Brigadier General Smallwood, Captain Bailey, and a few other trusted advisers Alex didn't know. He'd been hoping to spend more time with Abby, too, but again he was disappointed, for she took a seat near Locke and the other leaders. When she's wasn't listening to their conversations, she would put on a pair of old headphones and tune out to music, or else immerse herself in the books she'd brought. She wasn't unfriendly to him; she'd turn and catch his eye from time to time, even smiling once or twice. But she wasn't exactly friendly, either. It was pretty clear to Alex that she wanted to be left to herself.

Defeated, he even contemplated striking up a conversation with Iggy, but soon thought better of it. Things would have to get a whole lot worse before he'd try that again. Besides, Iggy had also pulled out his headphones shortly after getting on the bus, playing his Thrashtech and Synthipop favorites so loud Alex recognized every song. He, too, clearly wanted to be left alone.

Alex didn't blame either of them. So much had happened, and was about to happen, that they probably just needed time to process. When Alex thought about everything that had occurred in recent months—from Abby's dad's death and Alex's early run-ins with Locke, to the Best Band contest and their flight to the forest, their encounters with General Arnold, their capture in Hope and subsequent escape from Lincoln—it was surprising none of them had gone crazy.

As the bus continued its long journey, Alex thought about what lay ahead. They were nearing Washington, D.C., now. Soon they would enter America's great capital city and rendezvous with allies. Alex, Locke, Abby, Iggy, and their small team of soldiers would enter a tunnel leading to the secret underground entryway to the White House. There, General Arnold would let them in and together they would take over the MeChip control center, free the population of its insidious influence, and arrest President Davison. Once the area was secured, the true President, Francesca Delano, who would be waiting safely nearby, would arrive and broadcast to the nation. That was the plan, at least.

It sounded so simple. But would it work? For all Locke's reassurances, Alex still didn't trust Slade Arnold. And yet everything depended on this man. The whole mission—and the future of America—hinged on this traitor. Could someone that bad have truly turned good?

Alex looked out of the window again. They were finally entering the outskirts of the city. At first glance, Washington looked much like Lincoln; the streets were garbage-strewn, the sidewalks cracked. At a crosswalk, a group of people stood in silence, their complexions gray, their torn, stained clothes hanging off their underfed bodies as they waited listlessly for a rusted, fume-spewing car to pass by. A few blocks away, two smokestacks belched out black soot, thickening the layer of smog that hung above the neighborhood.

Alex was surprised. He remembered learning in class that Washington was beautiful, a towering monument to modern America.

Was it all like this? The bus slowed, bumping over potholes as the traffic grew heavier.

As they crested a hill, however, a shimmering light suddenly penetrated through the window. Momentarily blinded, Alex rubbed his eyes, then looked again. It was hard to make out what it was at first. Up ahead was something big and so bright Alex had to squint and look away. What was it? It was far too low in the sky and too early in the afternoon for it to be the sun. Shielding his eyes with one hand, he strained once more to see it clearly. Finally, he recognized it for what it was.

An enormous dome. It spread out before them, covering the entire heart of the city, its surfaces sparkling and glistening, iridescent in the sunshine.

They had finally arrived.

35 | The Checkpoint

Alex gasped as they drew ever closer and it dawned on him how vast the dome really was. It rose above them like a mountain, its highest point lost in cloud. The traffic slowed down further and Alex saw a checkpoint ahead controlling entry into the massive structure. Regs were stopping every vehicle, evidently scrutinizing documents.

"Do not worry," Dr. Locke said as he stood and made his way slowly up the aisle towards the back, finally sitting beside Alex. "All our documents are in order," he assured everyone.

"But be ready for action, just in case," Brigadier General Smallwood added.

"Why did you move further back?" Alex asked Locke.

"Just a precaution, in case some of the Regs have seen my mug shot. I'm a dangerous criminal, remember?" he smiled.

Finally, the bus made it to the front of the line. The driver pressed a button and the door opened with a *swoosh* as Locke shifted a little lower in his seat. Two Regs boarded, both with laz-rifles hanging from straps.

"Papers, please," one said.

"Here we are, officers," Brigadier General Smallwood said. "I think you'll find everything's in order."

The Reg scanned the papers.

"This looks fine. Wait, what's that?" He pointed at something on the page.

"Our Dome secondary passcode," Smallwood replied. "Is there a problem?"

"That's last week's number. They don't start with "V" anymore."

"Oh? Are you sure?"

"Yeah, I'm sure," the Reg answered, sounding irritated. "We're gonna have to pull you in for questioning. You'll all have to disembark."

Alex acted without thinking.

"Turn my MeChip back on," he hissed at Locke.

"What?" Locke whispered back.

"Turn it back on. Just for a minute."

"It may be detected."

"We have to take the risk."

After a moment's hesitation, Locke pulled out his remote and pressed several buttons. The millisec it started working again, Alex sent his MeChip into overdrive, his mind reaching into those of the Regs:

The papers are in order. The papers are in order.

"As I was saying, you'll have to ... wait ..."

"Is everything alright, officer?" Smallwood asked, frowning.

The papers are in order. Everything is fine. The papers are in order, Alex persisted, trying to stay calm and composed as he sought to exert control.

"Yes, everything is ... fine," the Reg said at last, his frown clearing. "The papers are in order."

"They are?" Smallwood asked, sounding surprised.

"Yes, the papers are in order."

"The papers are in order," the second Reg parroted.

You may enter the Dome. You may enter the Dome.

"You may enter the Dome," the two Regs said in unison.

On your way.

"On your way."

The Regs disembarked and the bus slowly accelerated away. Locke instantly switched off Alex's MeChip and turned to the others on the bus, telling them briefly what had just happened.

"We owe you a debt of gratitude," Francesca Delano said, smiling at Alex as soon as she'd heard Locke's explanation.

Alex nodded shyly. He was about to reply when everyone's attention was drawn to what was outside. Alex followed their gaze as they looked out of the windows.

They were entering the Dome. And everything had changed.

36 | The Shining City

The inside of the Dome was as different to the outside as a flamingo is to a dung beetle. The street broadened into a tree-lined avenue flanked by grand period homes, each fronted by picket fences and pristine gardens. As the bus advanced further in, Alex passed an open park of green grass, cherry blossom trees, and flower beds sporting a riot of colors; a café and various elegant-looking shops; and modern, luxury apartment buildings, their gleaming windows sparkling in the sun. The people striding the sidewalks seemed vigorous and healthy. The air was clear.

"Welcome to the Dome. This is the center of everything; the playground of the elites," Dr. Locke said, his face grim.

"This is how we all should live," Alex replied, unable to believe what he was seeing.

"This is how we all *will* live if our revolution succeeds," declared Francesca Delano. "I promise you."

They parked on a quiet street at the rear of a building with scaffolding and 'Museum Under Renovation' signs.

"The White House is just a few blocks away," Locke explained.

As Alex entered the building, it was clear they had friends even here in the Dome. After passing through security and a group of construction workers keeping up a pretense of renovating the old museum, they finally entered the inner sanctum of offices and rooms running the resistance movement inside the Dome. Alex caught sight of dozens of people hard at work, peering at computer screens or bustling here and there on important business. Armed troops guarded the corridors and doors.

"I didn't know so many people here were on our side," Alex commented to Locke as they were led along a corridor by a soldier.

"We have friends in the Dome, yes. But don't be fooled. For each freedom fighter who has secretly joined our cause, President Davison can boast a hundred MeChip-controlled underlings. And many of the elites will not give up their power without a fight, either. We are still seriously outnumbered."

They went over the plan once again, talking through every detail. They would enter the tunnel, which was conveniently located in the basement of the old museum, at 7:20 a.m. tomorrow morning, disable anyone they encountered, and meet with Arnold at the hidden entrance at 8 a.m. sharp. He would let them in and they would make their way to the main MeChip control center underneath the White House.

"Why are there only us and six soldiers on this mission?" Iggy asked, looking around him. "I mean, check out all the troops we have here. There must be, what, a couple of hundred in the building? I say we bust in with our whole army."

Alex didn't like to admit it, but he wondered if Iggy had a point. Why was such a small force involved in such a critical mission?

"The MeChip control center is usually only lightly guarded," Locke explained. "Most of the President's forces are above it in the White House, or else scattered around the grounds and the city. With any luck, even their token force in the MeChip headquarters will be distracted by news of the attacks our friends will be making around the country."

"When are those happening?" Alex asked, thinking of his friend Tom, whom he knew would be involved on the assault in San Francisco.

"At exactly 6 a.m."

"Then why do we have so many soldiers here in the Dome? Are they just for decoration?" Iggy asked, nodding towards the troops coming and going outside their office.

"Once we have disabled the population's MeChips, our troops stationed in Washington will seize key strategic points around the Dome."

"Like what?"

"Capitol Hill, the Heptagon, the White House, the government media center … a few other places."

"And you're sure this tunnel will actually get us inside the MeChip control center?" Iggy asked.

"Your father said it would, and I trust him."

"Me, too," Iggy agreed quietly.

"Excellent! I knew we'd agree on something in the end," Locke replied to Iggy with a smile.

Alex watched Locke and Iggy with interest and concern. Did Iggy really trust his father now, or was it just wishful thinking? For a millisec, Alex was tempted to ask Locke what they would do if Arnold turned out to be a traitor? But what was the point? The answer was obvious enough. They'd lose. And the rebellion would be crushed.

"And now, I suggest we get some sleep. We will need to be on our toes tomorrow," Locke announced, interrupting Alex's depressing thoughts and worrying suspicions.

"Are you quite certain, Charles?"

"Yes, ma'am. He's shielding his calls. Against your explicit orders."

"That doesn't mean he's joined them. Perhaps he's—I don't know—emotionally involved with someone and wants it kept private."

She ran a hand through her platinum blonde hair, pouting slightly as her gaze dropped down to the plush carpet.

"One of my people overheard his conversation. This was no affair of the heart. Davora, we need to face the unfortunate truth. He has betrayed you." General Charles Tarleton's voice was gentle but firm.

President Davison did not reply for a long time. She sat unmoving, her eyes now fixed on one of the two American flags that adorned her office. Sighing deeply, she rose from her chair. She ran a hand through her hair once more, picked a tiny piece of lint from off of her perfectly-pressed aquamarine biz-suit, and turned her attention back to her handsome subordinate.

"Very well," she said at last. "We have no choice but to act. General, you know what to do."

General Charles Tarleton nodded and crossed the room, careful to conceal a smile of satisfaction as he closed the door quietly behind him.

Alone, President Davora Davison stood quite still. She did not move as a single tear appeared in the corner of her eye, glistening in the spring sunshine that lanced into the Oval Office.

Finally, as if remembering where she was, she brushed it away.

"Such a waste. Such a tragic waste," she said under her breath. She sighed again, shook her head slowly, then drew herself up to her full height, her jaw suddenly set. "But no one betrays me. Not even you, Slade." Her voice was still quiet, but now it was also full of anger ... of menace.

Striding back towards her chair, she flipped a switch and spoke into a small device on the desk, her voice no longer sentimental or even bitter, but businesslike once more.

"Edward, send for Captain Cornelia Cornwallis straight away. I'd like to tell her personally that she's just been promoted."

37 | The Patrol

Alex peeked around another corner. Again, there was no one there. So far, the underground corridors were completely clear.

"Empty," he said, turning to the others. "John, were you expecting anyone to be here?"

"Slade said they run occasional patrols, but they're rare."

"What was all the training for, then?" Iggy asked, sounding frustrated. "What's the point of getting ready for something that will never happen?"

"There's always a chance—"

He stopped as one of their soldiers held up a hand in warning. The group froze, listening. A moment later, they heard voices in the corridor ahead.

"I still don't get why we're down here."

"I told you, they're calling out everyone: us, National Guard, Fixers, everyone. Some sort of emergency."

"If there's an emergency it won't happen down here. What's the smeckin' point in dragging us out of bed for this?"

"They're just covering all the bases, Frank. Our new boss is being extra cautious."

"Why?"

"Doesn't want to end up like the last guy."

The voices were close now, their footsteps reverberating along the concrete tunnel walls. Locke motioned to Alex, pointing to the back of his neck while pressing buttons on his remote. A millisec later and Alex felt his MeChip switch back on. Instantly, he began to reach out with his mind, his MeChip worming its way insidiously towards their adversaries' devices. He detected their MeChips and held up two fingers to the group so they would know how many enemies were ahead of them. Using his MeChip, Alex began to communicate with those of his two foes.

There are people around the corridor. There is no need to worry. They're friends. All friends. You're supposed to meet them here and help them.

The footsteps faltered.

"I think our friends are nearby," one of them said after a pause.

"Yeah ... yeah, you're right."

"Let's check."

They turned the corner and Alex saw two Regs; a woman and a man. The man's peaked cap was slightly askew, several of the buttons on his black leather jacket were undone and his shirt was untucked, as if he'd dressed in haste. Each had a baton and pair of handcuffs hanging from their belts, with the standard-issue Mark 2 laser pistol nestled in its holster.

We're friends. We need to borrow your guns. Hand them over to the old man, please.

The man drew his weapon and handed it to Locke, who passed it to Abby. The woman began to do the same, then paused.

"I'm not sure about this," she began, holding her gun uncertainly.

We're friends. Give your gun to the old man.

"No, I don't—" She was clearly going through some internal struggle, her hand holding the gun was visibly shaking, when her eyes took on a glassy look and her head slumped down. Locke had used his remote on them both. Instantly, the soldiers on their team disarmed her, handcuffed and gagged them, then sat them down on the ground. Neither resisted.

"You should let me use my MeChip next time," Iggy said to Locke as they made their way slowly down the corridor. "Franklin couldn't get them under control properly. I'm better at it than him," he said, casting a contemptuous glance at Alex.

"No, Iggy. You will get your chance later, but right now Alex is in charge of mind control."

"But—"

"Iggy Elgar, this is not the time." John Locke gave Iggy such a withering look the teenager didn't reply, although he clearly wasn't happy.

They continued to walk in silence, stopping frequently to listen for noises ahead. For the next few minutes, though, all was silent.

"John, why did you turn my MeChip off again?" Alex asked, realizing it was no longer functioning.

"To limit the chances of detection. I've programmed all our MeChips with some protective programming, but it's not foolproof. We don't want to be spotted now, so the less we use them, the better. I'll turn everyone's on once we meet Arnold and enter the enemy's control center."

"One of the Regs said they'd called out all their troops," Abby said. "Did you expect that?"

"Yes."

"But doesn't that mean there'll be more people to fight?"

"Possibly. But they're unlikely to be down here. Most will be spread out on the surface. They'll be disorganized, too. According to Arnold, they have not trained for such an emergency in a long time. We believe a full mobilization will actually slow down their response time. Plus, when we turn off their MeChips, we expect many to be confused and ineffective. Some may even join our side."

Abby was about to speak again when one of the soldiers on their team lifted a hand for silence. Once again, the group froze, listening intently. Several voices were audible up ahead.

They edged closer to the corner and once more Alex felt the familiar tingle in the back of his neck as Locke turned his MeChip back on.

Alex reached out with his mind once more, the thin strands of invisible light stretching out towards his enemies. He strained to connect with them, seeking out their MeChips, ready to enter them and exert his influence.

There was nothing.

Frowning, he tried again, probing forward, intensifying his efforts.

"What's wrong? Are you inside their MeChips yet?" Locke hissed, noticing the look of consternation on Alex's face.

"No," Alex said at last, his heart racing with the effort.

"Why not?"

"Because they don't have any."

38 | The Elites

"Are you sure?" Locke asked quietly, frowning.

"Absolutely," Alex whispered back. "What should we do?"

"Use our laz-pistols. Sergeant Smith, will you take the lead? Weapons to stun, please. And be cautious. If they don't have MeChips, they may be part of the President's elite guard."

Sergeant Smith nodded, motioning for her troops to follow. They crept forward silently, weapons raised, as Alex, Locke, Abby, and Iggy stood aside. Alex noticed that whoever was ahead of them had stopped talking.

Sergeant Smith took a deep breath, then stepped out into the corridor.

Fzzoom! Fzzoom!

Two laser beams blasted into her chest, smashing her backwards. Her troopers advanced over her fallen figure, firing back. One of her colleagues fell, then another.

"Come on," Alex said, leading Locke, Iggy, and Abby into the fray as they rounded the corner and joined the shootout.

One of their foes had already fallen, a second and a third dropped under Locke's unerring aim. The last, seeing he was totally outnumbered, reluctantly dropped his weapon and raised his hands in the air. Locke, Alex, Iggy, and two of their remaining troopers advanced on him, covering the man with their weapons. He was dressed in dark green combat gear, golden eagle epaulets on each shoulder.

"What are you smiling for? We beat you," Iggy said, noticing the man's odd grin.

"You didn't, boy. I already called the Colonel. She's sending back-up."

"No way," Iggy shot back dismissively.

"Believe it or not, I don't care. But you'll be surrounded and outnumbered within minutes. You might as well surrender to me now."

Before Alex or the others could stop him, Iggy had raised his weapon and blasted their enemy in the chest. The man's grin faded and he grunted, staring down at his smoking chest, then slid to the ground, eyes closing as he fell.

"What? He had it coming to him!" Iggy said defensively as Locke looked at him disapprovingly. "Besides, my gun's set to stun, like we agreed."

"How are Sergeant Smith and our other troopers?" Locke asked, turning away from Iggy and addressing Abby, who'd been checking on their three fallen comrades.

"They're ... dead," she said, sounding shocked. "The enemy's guns were set to kill."

There was silence as the news sank in.

"Smeckin' monsters," Iggy muttered.

"Was he telling the truth about calling in more troops?" Alex asked at last.

Before Locke could reply, there was a crackling sound and a voice rang out from a walkie-talkie on their fallen foe's belt.

"What is your status, corporal? Repeat, what is your status? Over."

Without waiting, Alex picked up the walkie-talkie and spoke:

"All fine here ... um ... Colonel. Nothing to report," he said, trying his best to mimic the man's deep voice.

"What about the noise you heard? Over."

"That was a mistake. Just ... um ... rats. Over."

There was a pause. Finally, the voice spoke again:

"Who is this?"

"It's Corporal Henshaw," Alex replied, spotting a name tag on the man's chest and thinking quickly.

"Stay where you are, Henshaw. I'm sending a team down to join you now. Cornwallis out."

"Do you think she believed me?" Alex asked, looking at the group.

"Are you kidding? Of course she didn't!" Iggy retorted, rolling his eyes.

"Whether she did or not, more soldiers will be on their way. We should leave here immediately," Locke announced.

"Do we carry on the mission or abort?" one of their remaining soldiers asked.

"Carry on," Locke, Alex, Abby, and Iggy all said at once.

"What about the others?" Abby asked, her eyes flicking back to their fallen comrades.

"We must leave them. Time is of the essence. Once this is over, we will make sure they are honored with a proper burial."

Locke, Abby, and Alex quickly secured their unconscious enemies with their own handcuffs, then Locke led them onwards. They made their way down the corridor, which turned right and carried on for a long time. Finally, they arrived at an intersection. This time, Locke led them to the left. They continued, still meeting no one until Locke abruptly halted. On the right-hand side of the corridor, hardly noticeable in the concrete wall, was a small metal door.

"This is it," Locke announced, turning to face the group. "This is the secret entrance where General Arnold will meet us."

"How soon?" Abby asked.

"It's 7:57 now," Locke replied. "He should be here in three minutes."

"We'll secure the corridor," one of the three remaining soldiers said, heading in one direction and taking a position about fifty paces away, weapon at the ready, while one of her colleagues retraced his steps and did the same the other way.

"What now?" Alex asked finally.

"We wait," Locke replied.

"And hope the enemy doesn't find us," Iggy added.

They waited for one minute, two, three. At 8:00 they stared expectantly, watching the small door and listening for sounds from the other side.

Nothing happened. Time passed while they waited some more. Alex could feel his heart beating rapidly in his chest as the seconds continued to tick away with agonizing slowness. He stared at the locked metal entrance, willing it to open.

Still nothing.

"What's the time now?" Iggy asked for the third or fourth time.

"8:06," Locke replied, his brow furrowed.

"What's going on? Where the smeck is he?" Iggy asked, looking as worried as Locke.

"Come, Slade. You might as well tell us everything. We know the truth anyway." Her voice was cajoling, her cold blue eyes locked on his as she tilted her head to one side. A single strand of blonde hair fell across her face but she ignored it. Slowly she drew on her cigarette, held the smoke in her mouth, then let it filter out from her nostrils.

"I told you, Davora. I don't know what you're talking about. Whatever Tarleton said, it's a lie." General Slade Arnold's voice sounded as deep and calm as ever. But his appearance had changed almost beyond recognition. Secured by leather straps to a metal chair, his greatcoat and shirt were gone and there were dark bruises and several deep cuts on his chest and biceps. A close observer would have noticed small puncture wounds on his forearms. His left eye was badly bruised and partially closed. Traces of dried blood were visible under his left ear and across his chin.

"Slade, we know each other too well for this," President Davison said, walking around the side of his chair and leaning close to whisper in his ear. "I can always tell when you're lying, old friend. You know I don't want to do this. Tell me the truth and I can make it easier on you."

General Arnold's eyes darted around the room. It was all metal surfaces except for the concrete floor and a darkened window which, he knew, led to a viewing area where others could watch the interrogation unseen. Several soldiers stood impassively around the room's perimeter, weapons holstered, eyes watching him for movement. But there was none. He was completely secure, unable even to raise a hand in self-defense. There would be no escape from here, he realized grimly. He'd been betrayed and his plans had failed. No one was coming to save him.

A walkie-talkie crackled and a red light started pulsing on the small device hanging from the belt of one of the watching warriors.

"Colonel Cornwallis, kindly take your business outside," President Davison said dismissively, a note of irritation in her voice.

"Yes, President," she replied, hastening from the room and closing the door firmly behind her.

"This is your last chance, Slade. Come now. Tell me the truth. After everything we've been through together, so many memories we've shared, it's not too late to put things right. I can forgive you, even now," she said, leaning in to whisper in his ear, her voice deep and husky. "Think of everything we can still achieve together. Slade, please ... come back to me." She walked round to stand in front of him, drawing slowly once more on her cigarette and bestowing on him her most winning smile.

For a moment Arnold was seized with an almost overwhelming desire to admit everything, to beg her forgiveness. But just for a moment. He could not turn back. Not now. Besides, she was lying. He knew that. No matter how close they had once been he knew she was ruthless and unforgiving to anyone who let her down. He had seen it too many times in the past. No one who betrayed her had ever been forgiven before. She would never change. Not even for him. No, he would just have to brazen it out and hope for ... what? A miracle? But that, he knew, was impossible.

"I have no idea what you're talking about, Davora," he said, trying desperately to sound convincing. "Ask Tarleton to show you the evidence. He's just making it up to get rid of me. He sees me as a rival for your favor, Davora. You know that."

For a millisec, a shadow of doubt crept across her eyes. Then she smiled once more.

"I've seen enough evidence, Slade. I know it was you. And if you won't talk then I'll have to make you talk; make you suffer."

Suddenly businesslike, she took a step towards him, the end of her burning cigarette pointing towards his face.

"Davora, don't do it," he said, speaking faster now. "I'm innocent. Please. You'll regret it."

"I don't think so, Slade," she said. The last thing he saw was the red tip of the cigarette as it reached his left eye.

Only then did he begin to scream.

39 | Someone Else

"**W**e have to face the truth. He's betrayed us," Alex said at last.

"He has not," Iggy shot back. "Something must have delayed him, is all."

"Whatever happened, the fact is we cannot get in," Locke pointed out.

"Are you sure? Can't we just—I don't know—blast it open or something?" Iggy asked.

"The metal is too thick. And there's no handle on this side. It can only be opened from within," Locke replied in a resigned voice.

"Then what do we do?" Abby asked.

"We will have to retrace our steps before more troops arrive."

"Then we've failed?" Iggy shook his head in disbelief. "No way. There must be—"

"What was that?" Alex asked, interrupting him and holding up a hand for silence.

"What?"

"That noise?

The group was silent once more. For a moment, Alex wondered if he'd imagined it. Had it been a trick of the mind, a delusion born of desperation? Then it came again; a creaking sound. And it was coming from the other side of the door.

"He made it! I knew he'd come," Iggy said triumphantly, a huge smile spreading across his face.

"What if it's not him?" Abby asked.

"Everyone step back. And have your weapons ready, just in case," Locke warned.

They stood there, laz-pistols raised as the door creaked again. Without warning, it began to move, opening outwards towards them, its hinges squealing in protest. Then a figure stepped out into the corridor, head bowed as she clambered through the small opening. She was in military fatigues and the insignia of a colonel was on her arm. Her shoulder-length brown hair was tied back in a bun and her laz-pistol was still in its holster.

"Don't shoot!" she cried out, her brown eyes wide with alarm as she saw seven weapons trained on her. "I'm a friend!"

"A friend of whom?" Locke asked, his voice stern. "Tell the truth, now."

"Of General Arnold. I'm Captain Cornelia Cornwallis. Colonel now, I guess," she added, as if she'd momentarily forgotten. "And you are John Locke," she said, her hands still held up in a sign of surrender. "He's told me all about you."

"Well, he shouldn't have," Locke said, his voice still hard-edged, his weapon still aimed at her.

"He had to. I joined him some time ago, but I only knew my part of the plan. He only told me the truth about you yesterday after he caught wind of his impending arrest."

"And what did he tell you to do?"

"He told me to come here at 8 a.m. and let you in. Then he said I should bring you to the MeChip control center and help however I can."

"I see. And did he tell you anything else?"

"Yes. He told me the password."

"And it is?"

"*Family forever.*"

"Then it seems we must trust you," Locke said, lowering his weapon at last.

"Good. Follow me."

"Wait. Where's my fa ... I mean, where's Arnold?" Iggy asked.

"He in the interrogation center under the White House. It's two levels above the MeChip control center."

"Is he okay?" Iggy asked, his voice oddly high-pitched.

"No," Colonel Cornwallis admitted, unable to hold Iggy's gaze. "They've been torturing him."

"Then we need to go rescue him right now!" Iggy insisted.

"We can't," Locke replied. "Not until we have secured the MeChip control center. When we do that, we can gain control of people's MeChips."

"So what?"

"With the exception of her special guard and some of her officers, most of the President's troops are under the MeChip's influence. We need to gain control of their MeChips—or at the very least, we need to disable them—before we do anything else. Once we achieve that, we will have a fighting chance of freeing Slade Arnold."

Iggy opened his mouth, shut it again, then nodded.

"Fine! But let's hurry."

After pulling the metal door closed and locking it again, Colonel Cornwallis led the way up the tunnel. It was narrow and had obviously not been used in many years, with cobwebs hanging from the ceiling and dust coating the floor. The only illumination came from two flashlights, one carried by Cornwallis, the other by Locke. Their progress was slow as they moved awkwardly and in single file, hunched over to avoid hitting their heads against the low ceiling. Finally, they reached another small metal door. Cornwallis pushed against it and it opened, its rusty hinges squeaking loudly.

They entered a dimly lit storeroom. It looked almost as unused as the tunnel. Judging by the dust trails on the floor, Alex guessed that several large crates had recently been shoved aside to reveal the door.

"Does anyone else know about this tunnel?" Locke asked as they moved towards another, larger door.

"I don't think so. I'd never heard of it and it's not on any of the plans. How Arnold found it is beyond me," Colonel Cornwallis admitted. She turned the handle and pushed, revealing a corridor occupied by three soldiers in uniforms similar to her own.

"Stand down," she instructed them and the three men lowered their weapons. "These are three of my most trusted troopers," she said, introducing them to Alex and the others. "They've joined our cause. And this is Dr. John Locke and his team. He'll tell us what we need to do now." She stood aside as the old man addressed them.

"First, we must secure the MeChip control center, and we must do it soon. Colonel Cornwallis, tell us everything you know."

40 | The Control Center

They advanced cautiously towards the MeChip control center, meeting and disarming at least two dozen guards on their way and leaving them all stunned and handcuffed. All were under MeChip control. After the first encounter, Locke switched on Iggy and Abby's MeChips so they could help.

"See, I told you I was great at this!" Iggy declared triumphantly the first time he used his powers to disarm a passing patrol.

"Yes, very impressive," Locke said as they handcuffed and gagged the men, leaving them sitting on the ground before moving on.

Finally, they approached a door where two more soldiers stood guard. Colonel Cornwallis distracted them while Abby used her MeChip to pacify them and Locke used his remote to render them unconscious. Again, they handcuffed and gagged them. All had agreed that they would never take an enemy's life unless they had no other choice. Their weapons were all set to stun.

"Ready?" Locke asked, turning from the doorway back to the others, who nodded.

"Let's do this!" Iggy answered, tugging on the door handle. A moment later and they were inside the control center.

It was a huge room, at least the size of a football field. Alex and the others were standing on a metal gantry about forty feet above the floor. It ran around the entire perimeter of the room, with stairs down to the main level at regular intervals. Immediately, the six soldiers on their team began to fan out around the gantry, taking up positions at regular intervals and looking down on the main level below. Colonel Cornwallis remained unmoving by the door they'd just entered, scanning the scene, weapon at the ready. Meanwhile, Locke, Abby, Iggy, and Alex walked quickly towards the closest stairs and began to descend to the main level. As he followed the others down the steps, Alex stared in wonder at the scene below.

There were rows of computers—Alex guessed there could be as many as a thousand in all. Many workstations were unattended, but there were at least 150 people there, some pacing up and down and checking monitors as they went, others seated and focused on a particular computer. In the center of it all on a raised dais was a much larger chair—almost like a plush, leather throne—and three huge screens. Someone was seated on the big chair, staring avidly at the monitors and occasionally manipulating the images with his fingers, which brushed the air in front of the screens.

No one noticed Alex and the others at first. All were so intent on their work that the soldiers under Locke's command were all in position and Alex, Locke, Abby, and Iggy were among the computers before anyone looked up. Finally, though, faces lifted and people began to talk, nudging each other and looking up at the gantry or at Alex and the others as they walked purposefully towards the center of the room. To Alex's surprise, though, none of them did anything to stop them. They just stood and stared.

It was only when they reached the dais that they met resistance.

"Yes, what is it?" asked the man sitting on the throne-like chair, without looking up. He was middle-aged and lean, his black hair graying at the temples. "I said what is it?" he repeated, aware of their presence but clearly unwilling to tear his eyes away from the screens. "Can't you see I'm busy here? Some of the regional sub-centers are down and we have several smaller outages in the system—possibly more—and I'm getting reports of sabotage and the daytime shift still hasn't arrived for some reason and I don't have time to ... oh."

He had finally raised his eyes. He saw Iggy's gun first, then Locke's grim expression. "But you're ... I mean ... you invented ..."

"Yes, I am Dr. John Locke and I did indeed invent all of this. And who are you?"

"Sinclair."

"Well, Sinclair, you are going to help me override the MeChip's control mechanism."

"But that will ... I can't possibly—"

"You can and you will. But first, I must speak to your colleagues here. Move out of the way, please."

Sinclair stood aside as Locke sat down. He stared at the screens carefully for several seconds, his eyes darting left and right.

"Let me see ... ahh, here we are." His left hand moved upwards in a sweeping motion and suddenly his voice amplified around the room.

"Colleagues, this is an emergency situation. Please follow Colonel Cornwallis through the entrance to your right. You will proceed directly to room B, where she will explain what is happening and give you further directions."

"But what's going—"

"There is no time to explain. Please file out of the door to your right. Quickly now."

With many backward glances the staff began to file away, directed by Colonel Cornwallis and two of her soldiers, who had descended to the main level. Within a couple of minutes, the room was empty except for their group, the four soldiers remaining up on the gantry, and a miserable-looking Sinclair.

"Now, Sinclair, show me how to access the control mechanism override. Is it—"

"What's going on here?" a voice shouted.

Alex raised his eyes and saw a soldier standing by a doorway on the far side of the room. As he spoke, a dozen more troops fanned out behind him.

"They're rebels. Stop them!" Sinclair shouted, pushing Abby aside and lunging for something behind his chair. A millisec later and he whisked around, laz-pistol in hand. But Alex was quicker, his stun shot blasting the man into unconsciousness.

Everything seemed to happen at once. The enemy began firing at them, forcing Alex and the others to take shelter behind the dais. Blasts of light smashed around the room and they returned fire. Their allies—the soldiers up on the gantry—began blazing away, too, dropping several of the enemy before they even knew what was happening. But there were still seven or eight adversaries left. Alex saw one of their own soldiers up on the gantry take a shot to the head. He fell against the railing and tipped over the edge, landing with a crash on a bank of computers below. Alex continued to return fire with his laz-pistol, hitting another foe. He would have used his MeChip on them if he could, but the range was too great. An enemy's shot smashed into the large chair in front of him, toppling it over. Then another of the soldiers on their side fell to enemy fire. Enraged, Alex fired back, catching an adversary in the shoulder and spinning him backwards.

Fzzoom! Fzzoom! Smash!

The large monitor on Alex's left cracked and wobbled on its base as a laser hit it head-on.

"What are they doing?" Abby yelled above the noise. "Don't they know what this is?"

Either they did not know or did not care, for a moment later a wayward blast struck the middle monitor, shattering the screen and making it crackle and fizz. Smoke began to plume up from the device as an ear-shattering alarm began to sound. Up above, a large red light on the ceiling started flashing in time with the deafening noise. The fight continued, but finally only one enemy remained. He began to back away shooting wildly, his laser beams spraying around the room, striking other computers. Alex saw him toss something in their direction as he turned and sprinted away.

"Move!" Locke bellowed as the object flew towards them. They dove behind the nearest bank of computers as the device struck the fallen chair. A millisec later and it detonated in an enormous explosion.

Alex huddled behind a desk with the others as shards of metal and plastic and glass flew overhead, raining down over half the room.

They waited several seconds before emerging from their hiding place. Alex coughed as the dust of the blast began to settle, looking around at the devastation. Smoke was pouring from the main monitors and at least twenty of the smaller computers were on fire. The alarm was still sounding, but Alex's ears were ringing from the explosion and it sounded more distant than before.

"What the smeck were they thinking?" Iggy shouted above the noise as he surveyed the damage.

"I don't think they were," Locke bellowed back. "I suspect they were simply slaves of the MeChip, programmed only to apprehend or destroy any enemy they encountered."

"Can we gain access to the MeChip control mechanism?" Abby asked uncertainly as she stared at the broken monitors.

"I don't think we have to," Locke replied.

"What do you mean?"

"I mean this was the control center for all MeChips. And since it has just been disabled, every MeChip in America will now be out of action."

41 | Slade Arnold

"Does that mean we've won?" Alex asked uncertainly.

"No. There are elites in the Dome and elsewhere who are not under the MeChips' control. Some may see the error of their ways, but others will be desperate to defeat us. And those whose MeChips have been turned off will be confused and scared. A few may help, but most are unlikely to be in any condition to assist. Some may even try to stop us," Locke said.

"So what do we do now?"

"We stick to our original plan as best we can. We have to secure the White House and capture President Davison. Once she's under arrest, I will try to hook up some sort of temporary device to communicate with the American people so we can explain what is happening."

"No! First, we free my father," Iggy insisted.

"Of course. You are right, Iggy. He is just above us in the White House basement."

At that moment, two figures appeared from out of the smoke: Alex raised his weapon, then lowered it. It was Colonel Cornwallis and one of her remaining soldiers who had descended from the gantry.

"What happened here?" she asked, eyes wide.

"Let's just say the MeChip isn't our biggest problem right now," Iggy replied.

"Are the control center staff secured?" Locke asked her.

"Yes, they're locked in a room nearby. Two of my men are guarding them."

"Good, then we must leave them for a while. Time to take the White House."

"With only six of us? That might be difficult," Colonel Cornwallis replied.

"We have to try. Besides, anyone with a MeChip will be in a state of confusion and our forces on the outside will soon join the attack."

"The President still has her elite guard."

"Yes. But we must try," Locke insisted.

"And we start by finding my father," Iggy said.

Colonel Cornwallis stared at him for a moment, then nodded. "We need to handcuff the soldiers we just stunned. Then, I can lead you to him."

"Wait here," Colonel Cornwallis instructed them as they stepped out of an elevator and into the White House's lower basement. "I'm going to scout ahead."

They stood in silence in the empty corridor, listening and watching.

Nothing happened. The alarm was still blaring and a red light pulsated in the ceiling. But there were no other people around. No sign of life.

"Why her?" Iggy asked at last.

"What?" Locke answered distractedly, his eyes still locked on the corridor ahead.

"Why does she get to scout ahead and not one of us?"

"I would have thought that would be perfectly obvious. Colonel Cornwallis is a senior member of the President's military staff. As far as we know she is not suspected of changing sides, so can advance unmolested. She also knows this building inside and out."

"If she knows it so well, why isn't she back yet?"

Locke did not even bother replying. A millisec later, the Colonel emerged from around a corner.

"The first part looks clear. I should be able to get us pretty close to where they're keeping Slade."

"Then why are we standing here?" Iggy asked.

Cornwallis led them up one corridor, took a right turn, then a left.

"Nearly there," she assured the group.

"Where is everyone?" Abby asked.

"I don't know," Colonel Cornwallis replied. "They can't all have dis—"

She paused as they heard a noise up ahead.

"I said remain in position!" a voice bawled from somewhere around the corner.

"No way. Something's seriously wrong. We're going up top."

Fzzoom! Fzzoom! Fzzoom!

There were screams, then silence.

Colonel Cornwallis motioned them forwards, keeping close to the wall as they advanced in silence. She peered round the corner, raised her gun, and fired. Alex and the others followed her around the corner.

There were four bodies on the ground, all motionless. Three were in regular combat fatigues, while the fourth was in the dark green gear of the President's elite guard.

"This is the one I just shot," Cornwallis said, nodding towards the elite trooper. "I think the others all had MeChips and were panicking now they'd stopped working." As she spoke, she put a pair of handcuffs on the unconscious elite guard's wrists.

"So he just killed them?" Abby said, shaking her head in disbelief and staring in disgust at their insensible enemy.

"We don't have time for this. Where's my father?" Iggy cut in.

Cornwallis led them on. Finally, they reached a metal door.

"He's in here," she said. "We should proceed care—"

But Iggy was already moving. Heedless of any danger, he tugged on the handle and hauled the door open, dashing inside. After a millisec's pause, Alex and the others followed him, guns at the ready.

Arnold was there, alone. He was secured by straps to a metal chair, his head slumped forward onto his chest. He wasn't moving. Alex gasped as he saw deep cuts and purple bruises on his body.

"Father ... Dad, are you okay?" Iggy rushed forward, his voice cracking.

"Let me check his pulse," Locke said, joining Iggy and placing two fingers on Arnold's neck.

"Is he—"

"He's alive. There's a heartbeat. Faint, but there," Locke said, as Iggy sighed in relief. "He needs medical attention."

Colonel Cornwallis dashed from the room, returning a moment later with a first aid kit and a bottle of water. She began to treat Arnold's injuries as Iggy removed the straps tying him down. Arnold groaned as he regained consciousness, raising a hand to his face.

"What's wrong?" Iggy asked.

"It's my eye," Arnold groaned.

"Let me see," Cornwallis said, taking charge.

Reluctantly, he removed his hand.

Alex gasped. Slade Arnold's left eye was gone. In its place was a lumpy mass of burned flesh, the skin charred and blackened beyond all recognition.

42 | The West Wing

"Hold still. This is going to sting," Colonel Cornwallis warned as she tended to Arnold's disfigured face.

"I thought you'd gone back to her side," Arnold grunted, looking at her from his remaining eye and wincing as she applied ointment to the wound.

"No, Slade. You were right. We can't go on treating our fellow Americans this way. It has to end. Now. Today." Colonel Cornwallis' voice was low but full of fire as she began dressing his wound with a bandage.

"Then let's do it," Slade Arnold said, rising with an effort from the chair.

"Dad, you have to rest," Iggy said. "I can take care of Davison. Get revenge for what she's done to you."

"I can rest later."

"But ... are you sure?"

"Yes, son. I'll be alright. Come on. Let's go."

They left the way they'd come, Arnold picking up the fallen elite guard's weapon and putting on his dark green jacket, which he said might cause enemies to hesitate before firing. He was not in good shape, though, and their pace slowed as Colonel Cornwallis led them down a side passage that eventually ended in a doorway.

"It's locked," Alex said, tugging on it. But the Colonel pulled out an old-fashioned swipe card and waved it in front of a sensor. There was a click and Alex pulled the door open, revealing a set of concrete stairs leading up.

"Old school," Alex said, regarding the swipe card with interest.

Colonel Cornwallis led them up one more level. There they paused. They could either continue up another set of stairs or try a door leading to the right.

"Where now?" Cornwallis turned to Arnold as he labored up the steps behind her.

"I think the door, don't you? You know what she does under pressure."

"The West Wing. Of course," Cornwallis replied as Arnold nodded.

"And that's where this door leads? To the West Wing?" Alex asked.

"Yes. There's a passage below ground that will bring us up under the old press offices."

Again, Colonel Cornwallis used her swipe card to open the door, leading them down another empty corridor. Finally, they reached some more steps, which they ascended, then another door, which the Colonel unlocked. They entered a room filled with old boxes and dust-covered computers. They were at ground level now and there were narrow windows looking outside onto a garden.

Whump! Boom! Whump!

Alex ducked his head instinctively as explosions erupted outside, shattering the glass in one of the windows. A moment later and laz-rifles started sounding in the distance.

"That will be the cavalry arriving," Locke observed.

Cornwallis led them through another door. With Locke and Arnold in the rear, she took them down a corridor and into a second room with doors at either end. Before they could all enter, though, armed troops began to pour in from the other side of the room. The woman at the front of the platoon pulled up short and lowered her weapon, looking uncertainly at Colonel Cornwallis and the rest of the motley band: Iggy, Alex, Abby, and Cornwallis' last remaining soldier. Arnold and Locke, meanwhile, were still a few yards further back in the room behind them, out of sight of the newcomers.

"What's your status, sergeant?" Colonel Cornwallis demanded, instantly taking charge.

"We're under attack, Colonel. And our MeChips have stopped functioning."

"Where's the President?"

"In the Oval Office."

"Who's with her?"

"I don't know. A captain in the President's guard sent us to ... to secure the rear of the West Wing. I think some of her guards are still with her. I'm not sure. She sent a lot of them outside to fight."

"Where's the rest of your company?"

"Some of them panicked when their MeChips broke. There was a ... a shoot-out with the President's guard. Colonel, what the smeck's going on?" she asked, her voice trembling slightly.

"No time to explain. Get your platoon down to the MeChip control center. You should find two of my soldiers guarding a group of technicians. Tell them I sent you and do whatever they ask."

"What about the troops attacking us from outside?"

"They're on our side."

"Then who's the enemy?" she asked, raising an eyebrow and clearly confused.

"The presidential guard, for one. If you encounter any you will apprehend them or, if there are too many, retreat in good order."

The sergeant stared at Colonel Cornwallis for a millisec, obviously bewildered.

"What are you waiting for?" Cornwallis demanded. "Dismissed."

"Um ... yes, Colonel," she said at last, advancing towards them.

"Not this way. Take the corridor back to your right."

The sergeant turned and retraced her steps. A millisec later and she and her troops were gone.

"Well done," Locke said quietly as he and Arnold emerged from behind the doorway.

"Thanks for staying hidden, Dr. Locke. It may have been a lot harder if they'd seen an infamous, hardened criminal like you. You know there are still wanted posters of you everywhere," Cornwallis said, smiling for the first time since Alex had met her.

"Why didn't you get them to help us?" Iggy interrupted before Locke could reply. "We could always use more firepower," he added as he looked at their tiny group, which now numbered just seven, including his injured father.

"Losing their MeChips has clearly confused the sergeant and her platoon. I'm not sure we could rely on them and I wanted to get them somewhere where they'll be safe and won't cause any further harm. Besides, they may be able to help my two troopers down below to keep the technicians under lock and key."

They advanced down another corridor while the sounds from outside intensified. Alex caught a glimpse through the windows of soldiers exchanging fire across the lawn. The lasers sounded a lot closer now, although they had encountered no one else within the building.

"The Oval Office is around this corner," Arnold said quietly. "Anyone care to sneak a peek and see what we're up against?"

Alex stepped forward and snuck a glance. There were half a dozen of the President's guard standing in front of a door, which one of them was just closing.

"Your orders are to stay here. I'm heading to the Roosevelt Room to see if Smith's still there, then to the MeChip control center to find out what's happened to Sinclair and his staff." The man who'd just spoken headed off down a different corridor without waiting for an answer, while Alex pulled his head back and whispered urgently to the group.

"There were six, but one's gone. Five left. What now?"

"We have no choice. We need to get in there and catch her," Locke said. "Do any of them have MeChips?" he asked Alex.

Once more, Alex tried to connect with the enemy chips as invisible light stretched from him, its thin tendrils of control seeking theirs. After several seconds' searching, he shook his head.

"They must be presidential guard," Locke confirmed.

"I agree," Arnold whispered. "We'll have to do this the old-fashioned way. Ready your weapons. We attack on three."

Alex raised his gun and took a deep breath.

"One."

He looked at the people around him and his eyes caught Abby's.

"Two."

He tried to give her a reassuring smile but his lips didn't seem to want to respond. Instead, he just nodded. His mouth felt dry and his heart was thumping.

"Three."

With a deep breath, he stepped out and began to shoot.

43 | The Oval Office

Three of the President's guard fell instantly, surprised by the ferocity of the attack. But these were not her elite troops for nothing. The other two fired back and Alex heard the grunt of Colonel Cornwallis's last trooper as he fell to their withering fire.

Alex and Abby shot one more, their laser blasts merging as it struck him down. Meanwhile, Locke had hit their final foe. He slumped against the door, eyes closing as he slid unconscious to the ground.

Colonel Cornwallis was already kneeling beside her last loyal soldier, but it was too late. All life had left him. She placed her fingers over his unseeing eyes, closing them gently and taking a deep breath to steady herself. Then she stood up.

Iggy was already advancing along the corridor and the others joined him, their eyes fixed on the doorway. Outside, the noise of battle dropped away for a few millisecs before returning with renewed fury. The sounds of lasers, shouted commands, explosions, and screaming were closer now than ever.

Alex reached out and tried the handle. It was locked. Colonel Cornwallis took out her swipe card and waved it at the door. This time, though, it didn't work.

"This may require less subtlety," Locke said. "Stand back."

Together, he and Arnold pointed their weapons at the entrance and opened fire. It took several shots, but finally the wood around the lock splintered and cracked. Iggy kicked at it hard, sending the door flying open as Alex, Arnold and Colonel Cornwallis burst in. Iggy, Abby and Locke were close behind.

As Alex entered the room, he had an immediate impression of opulence: a blue carpet that felt thick and soft underfoot, mustard-colored curtains, a couple of couches, and two large flags. But his immediate attention was all on what was directly in front of him. There was someone standing behind the famous Oval Office desk.

But it was not President Davison. A man in his thirties wearing a general's uniform was staring back at them. His handsome face was contorted in a malicious grin. A laz-pistol was on the desk in front of him. There was a slight movement off to one side and Alex noticed a second, shorter man standing in the shadows. He was slender and young, perhaps in his twenties. Dressed in a smart biz-suit, he was visibly shaking, eyes wide with fear as he stared at them.

"Where's the President, Tarleton?" Arnold snapped, his gun trained on the man behind the desk.

"That's General Tarleton to you, Arnold," he replied, his voice measured and calm.

"Where's the President?" Arnold repeated.

"Long gone," Tarleton said, his tone taunting now. "But she'll be back in a little while with an entire tank division. I'd start running if I were you."

"Edward, where's the President?" Arnold asked in a softer tone as he turned to the younger man in the biz-suit.

Edward took a step back and looked around him, as if surprised at being noticed. He was wringing his hands together and swallowing nervously, shaking even more obviously than before.

"Me ... but I don't ... that is ... I can't ..." His eyes darted back and forth, first to Tarleton, then back to Arnold, and finally at a spot near the door behind them.

Fzzoom!

Alex spun around as a shot rang out. President Davora Davison had stepped out from behind the broken doorway. She was holding a laz-pistol just inches from Abby's head. She grabbed the teenager, disarmed her and pulled her close, backing towards the door.

At the same moment, Locke fell to his knees, clutching his chest, and Alex realized with a surge of alarm where the President's first shot had struck.

Fzzoom! Fzzoom! Fzzoom!

He spun around again just in time to see Tarleton grab his gun from the desk and exchange fire with Iggy and Arnold. The enemy general's shot missed Arnold by an inch, but Iggy and Arnold's struck true, smashing the man backwards into the presidential chair. He sat quite still, head back and eyes closed, smoke rising from his chest. Arnold and Iggy span around to face President Davison as she held the gun to Abby's temple and started backing away through the open doorway.

"John!" Alex rushed to help Locke, who slid sideways, landing heavily on the thick carpet. Abby cried out as she saw her grandfather fall.

"Don't grieve for him, girl. He always was a meddling fool," President Davison declared, her scorn for them clear in every word, every syllable she uttered. "My father despised him for being so spineless. A conscience is a weakness, he used to say. And looking at you all, I see the same pathetic softness," she continued, looking around the group before her eyes landed last on General Arnold. "Even you, Slade. How disappointing you were in the end. Strength is what counts ... which is why *I* am President."

No one replied and after a moment's pause she continued: "I am going to leave now and you are all going to let me ... or the girl will die."

There was a flurry of movement as someone brushed by Alex's shoulder and ran past them into the corridor. It was Edward.

"He was always a miserable little coward, too," President Davison said contemptuously, her eyes flickering towards him for a millisec as he fled, before she turned her gaze back to the group. "Just like Locke. And now—"

But President Davora Davison never finished her sentence. Abby's head had been slowly sinking forward, as if she was about to faint. Now it suddenly snapped upwards and the back of Abby's skull struck the President full in the face, smashing against her nose. Her hold on Abby loosened as the teenager tore free, diving to one side and out of reach.

The President took a step backwards, one hand raised to her face, the other still holding the weapon. Blood trickled from her nostrils and through her fingers. Angrily, she raised her gun to fire.

"You'll pay for—"

Fzzoom!

President Davison's eyes widened in surprise. She took a single step forward and opened her mouth to speak. No sound came out. The gun slipped from her fingers. Before anyone could move, she fell face-first to the floor.

Behind her was Edward. He was standing in the shadows a little way down the corridor and was holding a small laz-pistol. The muzzle of the weapon was pointed at the place the President had been standing.

"I am not a coward," Edward said, his eyes fixed on the fallen figure, his voice so low Alex could barely hear him. "And you were a bad, *bad* person."

The young man placed his gun back in his jacket pocket, stared for a long moment at the group, then turned and walked hurriedly away down the corridor. A moment later and he was gone.

"She's dead," Colonel Cornwallis said, kneeling beside the President's body. But Alex was hardly listening. His attention was all on John Locke.

"Wake up, John. Please wake up," a voice that sounded like his own cried out.

Next to him, Abby was kneeling over the old man, too.

Locke's eyes opened, flickering in recognition as he saw them.

"Proud ..." he muttered. He tried to say more, to speak again, but the effort was too great. He drew a deep, shuddering breath and his eyes closed.

"No!" Alex shouted. "This isn't it. It can't be it. Someone, do something. Who knows CPR? We need a doctor. Now. Now!"

"It won't work," Slade Arnold said quietly. "The President's weapon was set to kill. He's gone, Alex. He's gone."

Abby wrapped her arms around the old man's body, sobbing uncontrollably as Alex kneeled and watched, seemingly unable to move. He suddenly felt numb and distant, as if he was watching the scene from very far away.

Colonel Cornwallis knelt beside them both, a hand on Alex's shoulder.

Alex saw Abby raise her head from Locke's chest, her eyes streaming. Colonel Cornwallis was speaking to them, her mouth was opening, but Alex couldn't understand what she was saying. They were only words; mere noises and sounds. They couldn't bring Locke back. Nothing could.

Alex stood up abruptly and looked around. Iggy was nearby but he looked away as Alex turned towards him. Alex saw the older teenager wipe something from his eye.

On the far side of the room, Slade Arnold was by the President's desk, busying himself at a small control panel and an intercom. After playing with the buttons for several seconds, Arnold leaned forward and began speaking. His voice rang out, loud and clear, amplified a hundredfold by speakers inside and outside the building.

"This is General Slade Arnold speaking to you from the Oval Office. The President is dead. I repeat, the President is dead. As senior military officer, I am taking temporary command of the White House. I order all troops to cease fire. I repeat, all military are to cease fire. Effective immediately. All personnel on *both sides* to gather in the front lawn in ten minutes. I repeat, both sides are to cease fire *immediately* and assemble at the front lawn at eleven hundred hours."

44 | President Delano

When Alex thought about it later, he knew he must have been there. He had hazy memories of General Arnold addressing thousands of soldiers, Regs, and civilians in front of the White House, explaining what had happened. He could dimly recall how most had obeyed his orders but some had resisted. He knew there had been sporadic fighting throughout the city but that their allies had managed to secure the White House and most of the other key locations within the Dome over the next few days. What's more, Alex had an odd feeling he had spent more time down in the MeChip control center, which somehow Arnold had managed to repair well enough for the rightful President, Francesca Delano, to broadcast a message to every American fitted with a MeChip. He, Alex, had been one of the fortunate few to witness history being made when President Delano had addressed the nation from the Oval Office, explaining that they had all been deceived by the Davisons, manipulated by their MeChips for more than 15 years, and that she had a plan to rebuild the country, a vision to make America what it should be: a bastion of democracy and a shining beacon of opportunity for all.

He knew he had been there that historic day, knew he'd played his part in the weeks that followed, when they were struggling to defeat their remaining enemies around the country. Indeed, he could remember being so busy he'd barely had time to think as he ran messages for the new President, joined the clean-up operation around the damaged White House, or helped round up members of the elites who refused to surrender their unearned privilege and power without a fight.

But none of it felt real. For Alex, it was more like a half-forgotten dream than reality, a film he'd seen so long ago he could hardly remember any of the details.

There was a great emptiness inside him, a yawning chasm since John Locke's death. Correction, since his murder. He could not believe the old man was not there with them, that he could not see for himself just what he'd achieved. Alex kept imagining what they'd talk about if he was still alive. He wanted to tell his friend and mentor that he had more than made up for any mistakes of the past; that without him this revolution would never have succeeded. He could imagine the old man's penetrating green eyes sparkling with joy as they spoke of the revolution's success and what they would do next. He knew John Locke's keen intellect, scientific knowledge and deep humility would have been incredibly helpful to the new President as she took up the reins of power.

The funeral had been the worst part. A state funeral with full honors for Dr. John Locke, inventor of the MeChip and hero of the uprising. A funeral held on a wet, windswept April day, the driving rain mingling with Alex's tears as he stood alongside thousands of others. A day of speeches by important people like President Delano and General Arnold. A day to celebrate the life of a man who had tried—and succeeded—in making up for past errors. A day Alex was trying very hard to forget, since it dredged up far too many memories and emotions for him to deal with right now.

After the funeral, Alex saw that Slade Arnold, too, was trying to make amends for his past sins. The man seemed to be everywhere at once, his left eye still bandaged as he worked around the clock. Grudgingly, Alex had to admit that he had been wrong about Arnold. He had not been a traitor, after all. Their revolution had needed Arnold just as much as it had needed Locke. But Alex didn't really care about that very much. Mostly, he just missed his old mentor. His old friend.

Epilogue

Much, much later, exactly 100 days after that fateful moment when John Locke had died and President Davison's reign of terror had ended, Alex finally saw his mom again. It was early evening on the Fourth of July and they were gathering in the Capitol to celebrate the rebirth of their nation.

Alex swallowed nervously as he looked out from the Lincoln Memorial at the crowd in front of him. There was a sea of people, an ocean stretching back to the Washington Monument and beyond. He was standing off to the right of the columns, behind the security barriers, when he caught sight of her being ushered in by a team of Regs. She ran up to him, hugging him so hard it knocked the breath out of him. Finally, she pulled back and looked him up and down, smiling and crying at the same time. She appeared older now, her hair graying around the temples.

"You've grown," she said at last.

"You haven't," he joked back, smiling for what felt like the first time in forever.

She wasn't alone. Her husband Ben was there, too, beaming as Alex embraced him as well.

"How's life in Lincoln?" Alex asked them.

"Hard," his mom replied. "There's so much to do. We'll get there in the end, though. But Alex, there's something you should know. Something we need to tell you." That familiar lopsided smile that she showed when nervous appeared as she looked at him. Alex waited for her to speak, but instead she turned and looked over her shoulder.

Alex followed her gaze and saw several familiar figures approaching through the crowd. General Arnold was walking towards them with Iggy, who was holding hands with Leah Mecon. Iggy's mom Alice was with them, too. She was smiling to herself and kept shooting glances at Slade Arnold.

Alex smiled at them all as Leah leaned in and kissed him on the cheek.

"What are you all doing here?" he asked.

"We're here to see you, of course. Aren't we Iggy?" Leah replied with a grin. Iggy didn't answer.

"But why?" he said as they all stared at him. "Mom, what's going on?" he asked, beginning to worry.

"It's difficult to know where to start," she said slowly.

"How about at the beginning?" Alex prompted.

"That would take too long," Iggy interrupted, "and I'm already getting bored."

"Alright, here goes. Alex, I recently found out I have family I never knew about, someone the MeChip had erased from my memory," his mom said.

"Okay ..." Alex replied. "What sort of family?" He was beginning to have an odd feeling about this.

"Alex, I recently found out I have a brother."

"A brother? But ... who?"

"That would be me," General Slade Arnold said, a faint smile on his face.

"Wait, what? No way! But ... how?" Alex asked, utterly confused.

"It's really quite simple. Slade and I are brother and sister. We moved here from England when we were kids. Our father was an engineer with the Bright Green Mining Company, you see, and—"

"But you're not English, Mom," Alex said, thinking back to something John Locke had started to say to him months ago, but unable to really believe it. "I'd know if you were English."

"I was really young at the time, barely out of diapers. I don't remember England at all. But Slade is eight years older than me. He was ... how old were you, Slade, when we came to America?"

"Twelve."

"Right. Which is why he still has a slight accent and I don't. And then he left for college at just 16, which might explain why the memory of him took longer to return when my MeChip was disabled ... right Slade?"

"Exactly."

"Hold on, you're saying you were younger than I am now when you went to college?" Iggy interrupted, looking at his father. "Way to go to make me feel inadequate."

"It was really John Locke who can take the credit for me entering university at all," Slade Arnold said. "Our families were close and he took an interest in me whenever he came back to Lincoln from college and work. He was the one who told my parents I had the potential to go far academically and that they should let me sit the entrance exams early to get into his old university. In fact, he encouraged me all the way through. He was a mentor and a friend to me for many years before we ... that is, before *I* let him down."

There was silence for a moment as Alex processed what he'd just heard. Everyone was staring at him, waiting for his reaction.

"Alex, are you alright?" his mom prompted him at last.

"I guess. I mean, it's great that you've found your brother at last. Are you happy about it?"

"Yes, I am. It's wonderful to have more family. But Alex, it means he's your family, too."

"So I guess you're my ... uncle?" Alex said, barely able to believe what he was saying.

"I suppose I am," Arnold replied, smiling properly at last.

"Then I'd better get some really good Christmas presents this year, because you have a lot to make up for."

"That's what I told him," Iggy agreed.

"It's nice to have one more family member, I guess," Alex said at last, his brain still reeling from the news.

"Two," Leah corrected him, still grinning.

"What?"

"Not one new family member. Two."

"What? Who ... oh ..." Alex said, trailing off as he realized what she meant. Alex turned to look in disbelief at Iggy. "So if Arnold is my uncle, then that makes you my ... cousin?"

Iggy didn't reply. Finally, he met Alex's gaze and nodded.

"Oh, smeck!" Alex said.

"Hey, don't think I'm thrilled about it either. You're still a dexter as far as I'm concerned, Franklin. But since families are supposed to stick together, I guess I'll have to tolerate you."

"That's the spirit," Leah said, kissing Iggy on the cheek.

"We should continue this family reunion later," General Arnold said, looking at his watch. "Alex, I think you have someplace you need to be."

"Oh, right ... *that*." Alex hugged his mom one more time, turned, and made his way backstage.

"Break a leg," Iggy shouted as Alex walked away. "Seriously, I want you to *literally* break a leg, Franklin!"

Alex was standing in front of the world. They were watching him. All of them. Millions upon millions upon millions. They were watching him on giant screens across the country; on MeChips now freed from tyranny; and in person in their hundreds of thousands, stretched out in front of him.

Could they see him shaking? Was he about to freeze again? And why had he agreed to do this in the first place, to play the Star Spangled Banner and other songs celebrating America's rediscovered freedom?

But it was too late to back out now. President Francesca Delano had already spoken into the microphone and introduced them to the American people. She had already told everyone about their role in fanning the flames of revolution, even about their musical talents. Music may not have defeated the MeChip in the end, she'd said, but it does have the power to help unite us, to bring us together as a nation once more. And what we need more than anything, President Delano had explained, was to come together and find common ground as we rebuild our country. The cheers were deafening, the moment overwhelming. But it was far, far too late now for Alex to change his mind.

He turned to the others. Sol was looking very serious as he held his bass guitar tightly. Tom was grinning, as he always did at gigs, sitting behind his drum kit and obviously amped up by the occasion. The fact that a million people were in the crowd only seemed to have pumped him up more. Finally, Alex looked at Abby as she stood poised and ready in front of the keyboard. He wished he'd seen more of her lately; wished they hadn't both been so busy. But now she held his gaze, nodding as if to say, 'you got this'.

Which was all the affirmation he needed.

"Ready, guys? Then let's go: one, two ... one, two, three, four!"

As Alex strummed the first chord his fears suddenly melted away. He wasn't going to freeze. And he wasn't going to mess up. He was going to do just fine. Better than fine. This wasn't something to fear. It was something to cherish. Something to remember forever. Music was wonderful. It had a power all its own. A power to unite people. To unite an entire nation.

Alex took a deep breath, opening his mouth to deliver the first line.

And the crowd went wild.

"That was un-be-smeckin-lievable!" Tom yelled over the noise as they gathered offstage thirty minutes later, the deafening screams of a million people still ringing in their ears. "You guys were unbelievable," he added, turning to them and high-fiving each of them in turn."

"You weren't so bad yourself, Thomas. We'll make a drummer out of you yet," Sol replied, unable to stop himself from grinning.

"That's almost a compliment!" Tom laughed. "We'll make an optimist out of *you* yet, my friend. Come on, let's find Sally and Harriet. They're in the green room, I guess." Sol moved to follow his friend, but Alex stopped as a hand touched his arm.

"Coming, Alex? Abby?" Tom asked, turning.

"We'll catch you up," Abby replied. Still grinning, Tom and Sol turned and walked into the semi-darkness in search of their girlfriends, leaving Alex and Abby alone backstage.

"Look," Abby said, pointing to a rope ladder nearby. "I saw this earlier and it leads up to a little balcony. Wanna check it out?"

"Um, yeah. Sure. Why not?" Alex replied, a little surprised.

"Good. Come on, then."

She led the way up the ladder, rising gracefully while Alex struggled behind her. Abby quickly reached the top and soon Alex saw the little platform above him. He reached out, but his hand slipped. For a millisec he thought he would fall, imagining himself crashing down onto the back of the stage below. Then a hand caught his. A moment later and Abby was pulling him up and to the left where his fingers found the safety of wooden planks.

"Thanks," he gasped as he drew himself onto the little wooden structure that sat above the rear of the stage far below. The platform was small and there was not much room for the two of them to sit as their legs dangled over the edge. As he breathed in, he caught Abby's scent, an alluring combination he remembered vividly from the handful of other times he'd been this close to her before. What was it? A mixture of flowers and peppermint, perhaps? Not for the first time, he wondered if she was wearing perfume.

Neither of them spoke as they looked out at the stage a little ways in front of them and far below. President Delano was speaking to the crowd again, but it was less loud back here than it would have been in front, where the giant speakers were facing.

Abby turned to face him.

"Remind you of anywhere?" she said, leaning in to speak in his ear so she could be heard above the noise.

Alex looked at her, noticing for the first time some tiny flecks of green in her deep brown eyes.

"I'm not—"

"My treehouse," she said, smiling. "Fifteen steps, tiny wooden platform ... just you and me," she said, her head tilted to one side.

His thoughts turned instantly to the last time they'd been in the treehouse together. It had been just before these adventures had begun, the evening before Abby's father had gotten sick at the barbecue. That night in the treehouse had been the first time he'd come close to admitting how much he liked her; the first time he'd suspected she might, just might, like him too.

"Do you remember what we were talking about, before I got that call on my MeChip and had to go?" she asked, still smiling.

"Um ... kinda," Alex admitted, suddenly glad his face was partially shadowed. He wouldn't have liked to guess how bright red he must have just turned.

"Let me remind you. I was saying that you really wanted me to be your girlfriend, and you were about to admit it. And later in the forest we started talking about it again, but again we were interrupted before you could tell me how awesome and smart and tidy I am and how you were desperate to date me. Am I right?"

Alex was about to reply when they were interrupted by a buzzing sound. Abby paused, pulling an old-fashioned smartphone out of her pocket.

"It's my mom," she said, looking at the display, "and this time, I am *not* answering it." She pressed the red button on the device, switched it off, and turned back to Alex once more.

"So where were we? Oh, yes. You were about to ask me to be your girlfriend. Right?"

Alex swallowed, summoning his courage. Then he had a moment of inspiration.

"Can I ask you, or can I show you?" he said, smiling back.

"Go on, then," she replied, biting her lip as he leaned in towards her at long last for their first ever kiss.

THE END

From The Author

Dear reader,

Thank you for entering the world of *Rock Happy*. For those wanting to read more from the *Rock Happy* world, a <u>fourth novel</u>, ***Rock Happy: Aftershock*** is due out in <u>September 2024</u>. As America rebuilds itself under a new President and free of the MeChip's grip, life has one more shocking surprise in store for Alex—a final secret that might just change everything.

You might also be interested in ***Rock Happy Short Stories***, three tales that take place a year <u>before</u> the events described in the *Rock Happy* novels. This prequel delves deeper into some of the key characters and reveals more about their backstories and personalities. There are a couple of surprises in here, too!

The *Rock Happy Short Stories* are completely **free** and **exclusive** when you sign up for my monthly newsletter. To access these free stories and my monthly news and offers, all you have to do is provide your email address at: https://chrisspenceauthor.com/contact.html

Finally, if you enjoyed this book, I'd be so grateful if you could leave an ***online review*** on the site of the retailer you bought it from. That way, other readers will know what you think. A link to the many retailers who sell my books is available from my website: https://chrisspenceauthor.com

As our hero Alex might say—thanks so smeckin' much!

Chris Spence

About the Author

From politics to rock bands, journalism to environmental advocacy, Chris draws on his past experiences to write intriguing fantasy and science fiction.An award-winning writer, Chris is currently working on his **Rock Happy** dystopian books and the **Skyrack Chronicles**, a fantasy series where the characters' favorite role playing game comes to life.Originally from England, Chris has since lived in New Zealand, New York, San Francisco, and Dublin, Ireland.

Read more at chrisspenceauthor.com.

www.ingramcontent.com/pod-product-compliance
Lightning Source LLC
Chambersburg PA
CBHW051231130726
47988CB00001B/298